INSOUCIANCE

Thomas Phillips

Spuyten Duyvil

New York City

Library of Congress Cataloging-in-Publication Data

Phillips, Thomas, 1969-
Insouciance / Thomas Phillips.
p. cm.
ISBN 978-1-933132-96-9
I. Title.
PS3616.H4775I57 2011
813'.6--dc23
2011035481

for Anna

And dying—to let go, no longer feel
the solid ground we stand on every day—
is like his anxious letting himself fall

into the water, which receives him gently
and which, as though with reverence and joy,
draws back past him in streams on either side;
while, infinitely silent and aware,
in his full majesty and ever more
indifferent, he condescends to glide.

Rainer Maria Rilke, from "The Swan"

ONE

I t's not pedophilia. No. It's not that at all. She is much too old and I, it could be argued, too young relative to her age, for what we're doing to be considered abject behavior. And to the persistent naysayer, the brooding moralist, I say, relax. Watch a good film. Take in the air. Breathe. Climb the hill that passes for a mountain at the center of the city and behold.

Hurting people, particularly the young, the infirm, the vulnerable, is repugnant to me. Don't do that, I think or say when witness to another's violence. There's so much good to behold, to enact, why waste time on violence, foul deeds? The unscrupulous politics of victimizers—they know who they are, even when not actively celebrating the triumph of brutality—I find unwise. There is very little to like in such people, their politics, their muscle, even though it's in them, I believe, the core good, the distance they may take from the violence on occasion.

It's easy to be jostled by the word pedophilia. Few words elicit such immediate tension, a tensing of the muscles, thoughts contract around the word, the seizing up of the body in mixed company, squinted eyes. A horrible phenomenon. So I won't repeat it. It really bears no relation to what we're doing together. But the question of why bring it up in the first place. People, the way they talk. Their violence with words, the politics of desire, as Bénédicte might say, her education well rounded and astute. And more immediately, the complexity of a triangle. Three ports of entry into a dynamic that can stand to be worked out. The prospect of hurting someone, quite far from my preference.

She sometimes bears a striking resemblance to an actress whose name I always forget. I'm terrible at that. She remembers everyone's name, especially actresses for whom she is occasionally mistaken. There's the one in particular. She ingests film—serious, intelligent film, I want to be clear—the way others dine, linger over dinner, one's lunch break, a daily practice. I, too, enjoy the cinema, though not to the degree to which she absorbs its stories, the striking imagery. She likes discussing them as soon as the credits roll unless the film is exceptionally thought provoking. In which case she likes to sit for a moment, ponder the significance of the film before talking. There is a kind of post-coitus calm, a calm reverie in her demeanor following such a film, I say to her.

And there, in the wake of that moment, in response to my observation, half joking, is when she most resembles the actress in my mind, the actress whose name always escapes me. Her simper that contains as much censure—I know her well enough to know—as acceptance and goodwill. The way it protrudes from between her strands of hair and indicts the world, or at least its representative at that moment. That's when I see the actress whose every film we've watched together, some more than once. And then I tell her so and the censure disappears. The edges of her lips move a bit closer to her eyes, emphasizing her cheek bones, she smiles, she is pleased, ironically, she no longer resembles the actress, to my thinking. But I am, in that moment, instantly reminded of her mother, who I also know.

You have to hold it like this, she says to me. Grip it here, scroll this way with your index finger. Tap it. Some electronic device. I hate them. She loves them. Now watch what happens. It's impressive, readily admitted. I had no idea we've become this technologically advanced. Extraordinary. I finger the device some more while she looks on knowingly. There's so much that she knows. She's quite up to date with the new but has solid credentials in what has preceded the current technologies. Books, thoughts. One of the reasons we get on so well, I've long suggested to her.

People at the café observe us, it seems to me, it always feels this way to me, and I'm happy that their collective energy is likely directed at my bumbling through technology, as opposed to some perceived transgression. Some projected horror. The waiter brings us our tea. She has taught me to appreciate tea rather than coffee. I've learned to judge, to look down upon people who require coffee in the morning. She taught me this. But really, it's just a joke between us, our shared judgment of others, those people who succumb to the cliché of requiring coffee to operate in the domain of others, or alone, on any given day. We both know that judgment equates to a kind of violence, which we both abhor. As one who used to drink coffee every morning, I can handle the caffeine of green tea at this time of day. She sips at something from Africa, non-caffeinated, it smells good, woody. She has poured an alarming degree of half and half in with the tea, so that the liquid meets the rim of the mug and

forces her to take a quick sip. There are things I teach
her as well, our relation allows for such reciprocity. It's
late in the afternoon.

In the early evening we go our separate ways, our
own distinct directions. Toward the same place, as it
happens. We arrive at different times, greet one another,
ah, hello, in the company of a third party, ask questions
to which we both have clear answers, about how each
of us is doing. We embrace. She is well, her work is
going well, she loves what she does. Me too. Things are
good for me, thanks. I've taken your advice and started
drinking green tea. Feeling a renewal of my energy,
fewer colds, no more coffee. There's a wonderful new
exhibit at the art museum that she should see if she
hasn't all ready. And the article on Camille Saint-Saëns
that you recommended when the three of us last met, it
was wonderful. Though as expected, I find his musical
conservatism and nascent existentialism tedious. I'm
happy, I say.

The other with whom we currently occupy an
elegantly designed room, the space of my shared home,
though I don't notice it at the time, maintains an air
of gravity during our extended hellos, standing at a
distance, emotional and otherwise, from the extended
greeting. She, the youngest in the room, notices this
gravity and will tell me all about her observation next
time we meet. The memory of having expressed my

happiness in that moment of the three of us sharing an insincere space will eventually feel compromised to me, in the sole company of this other, in the night, in bed.

But now I watch as the two women trade stories of her brother. She has a brother whose whereabouts are often unknown. Today they are known. He's taken hold of the reigns of his life once more, far from home, but safe, galvanized his faculties, entered back into the stream of people operating according to structure, he's a good man, I like him, when I see him. We're all pleased that he's out of the slump. The two women move to another room, giving me a chance to contemplate the sincerity of my happiness. The contours of its secret face. Its body, its voice that speaks to me and fornicates with me in the afternoons, rarely in the evenings, same for the mornings, we must contend with certain limitations. The afternoon is my time to embrace the wonder of a life whose splintered pieces, broken off from a core of goodness—I believe this about myself and others, this foundational decency—adhere to that good for a brief interim. The integrity gained during our afternoons together has a way of salvaging me from the wreckage of damaging another. It's never been my intention to hurt anyone.

As for her, we've discussed the subject beyond either of our capacities to bear it much longer. The discussion, I mean. The happiness, I can't ever imagine giving this up.

We dine together, the three of us, the way civilized families do. Our conversation is lively without being overly animated. Our opinions about various matters political, philosophical, current events. We return to Saint-Saëns. Anna doesn't specify her tastes in classical music, she knows what she likes and doesn't like when she hears it. She listens with amusement to our banter about Saint-Saëns. Her real interests, the sparks that drive her own life and its conversations, lie elsewhere. Her daughter, on the other hand, is very clear about the music.

The way the day announced itself could not have been any more perfect. Fresh air coming through the open window, it's not yet so cold that the windows must be sealed shut for all those months. My partner, Anna, awoke later than me, I'm an early riser, that hackneyed phrase. Bénédicte, her daughter, was likely still asleep in her own home. I brought Anna some breakfast in bed, also hackneyed, her juice, yogurt, toast. She thanked me with a kiss that was as thoughtfully articulated as it was ushered by the accomplice of undesirable breath. I love the way she is in the morning, breath and all, she can be lovely in the evenings as well, I love her, I love most things about her, the way she complements a beautiful morning, which currently reflects her own solemn beauty. We've shared this home, such mornings, for nearly twenty years now. We proceeded to talk about the day ahead, Sunday, what we might do, places to visit. Or a day inside, surrounded by the comfort of our possessions, familiar spaces, the day was open to us. She was there on the bed and I took pleasure in witnessing the nuances of her expression, her voice—the food was beginning to mask her breath—which I've come to know quite well over the years, the manner in which she inhabits her body. And I haven't tired of these nuances, as people do.

She rolled over on her back and began reciting a poem from memory. How odd, I thought, the way people do this. What an unusual thing for Anna to do. After all these years. Not that she's in any way culturally deprived. But I had no idea of her inclination to memorize poetry. A vestige, surely, of her youth, her particular education, which I can only imagine she undertook with the utmost seriousness. For a career, independence. And now, for poetry. The content of which I found difficult to follow, until I was struck by a line that sounded disgusted coming from her mouth, an ugly condemnation of life that contrasted her clear, linen white beauty—there really is a kind of minimalism to the person that is Anna, highlighted by such subtle gestures of colorful being, soft visage—that rang with a certain force against the otherwise delicate features of her voice, her carefully engaged reciting self. I contemplated the words as she continued to hold forth , and into the pause following the end of her recitation. Whereupon she looked at me and laughed, she grabbed me easily by the neck, spilt what was left of her juice, all over the bed, forcing our mutual laughter. Nothing like a minor accident to accentuate the effortless joy of a Sunday morning.

It was all going so well. One of those delightful collections of hours spent with a loved one, and I, a hidden witness to the privilege of loving two while joyously present with one. Some would call it a curse. And then came the phone call from her ex-husband.

I like her ex-husband. He's very much like their son, with whom he shares a propensity to disappear. Men. He's a coffee drinker. Our morning gave to the tension of a call between former spouses. I could only hear her side of the conversation, she didn't elaborate later. I'm more than content to be left out of their negotiations. But remain ever receptive to Anna's concerns when she cares to elaborate. There was no need to offer an explanation today, so we carried on with the morning, the trajectory of which continued to go undecided. The tension of the call actually accentuated the pleasure of our morning together. Anna and I felt each other's feet and took a warm bath.

Sundays are ours. They belong to Anna and me. Mondays constitute the beginning of a work week, as they do for many people, for Anna and myself, earning an income, as well as the possibility of afternoons devoted to unhindered love-making with Bénédicte in her apartment. Or observing café life in discreet sections of the city—we are, of course, merely a young woman and her mother's partner having tea—a pair of friends at the cinema. I could go on. I could keep talking about the euphoria of Mondays and the weekdays that follow. Because I am in love with Bénédicte—daughter, intellect, beauty, film connoisseur —and a man in love can go on, he can speak, and often does when given the opportunity, of the seemingly infinite sensation of pleasure that informs his being in the world, colors the windows of his sight after having spent part of the day, months, coiled around the intimate smells of another, he blabbers on. But an intelligent man also understands the ephemeral nature of his pleasure. He knows that one way or another it will come to an end. And that this experience of love's dénouement isn't altogether bereft of pleasure, or love. He knows that ephemerality is part of the infinite, struggle though he may to forget an inevitable separation. I'm like this. Last Saturday afternoon with Bénédicte, while Anna was off on an appointment, had been an exception in our weekly ballet.

The city erupts in summer. All of the festivals, the music, theater in the streets, dance, one dines on a terrace, rather than confined within the stuffiness of restaurant walls. Now, as we move headfirst into winter, autumn is merely a flash here, you can feel the people tightening in the cold, everything tapering off, expressions. You feel it at its most pronounced when traveling on the metro, in a bus, others sitting across from you staring into your shins, and only haphazardly, a bit angrily, into your eyes. I take pleasure in countering with a smile, often met with an intensification of the cold. Commuter anthropology. Or when your shoelace comes undone and slithers through the dirty ice, sidewalk snow, you have to reach down, a chore in itself with layers of clothing, a bag over your shoulder, you're late, and then your bag slips and gets wet, the edges of your coat. The inner lining of which, perhaps a silk/goose down combination, nevertheless generates much appreciation when considered, its style, warmth. I love the extremity of cold, in relative moderation, and my coat is very fine indeed.

My closest friend, another woman, as it happens, has mixed feelings about Bénédicte. She just called me at work, quite out of the blue, as she sometimes does, to say that I should have my testicles surgically removed. Or bitten off. Then she called back, apologized. She explained that she is happy for me, and for Bénédicte, whom she knows and likes, but feels an unacceptable degree of stress regarding the potential suffering—we both know that potential is a comforting but unrealistic word—on the part of Anna, whom she also knows and holds in very high esteem. Anna once helped Lucille through a challenging episode. A dying parent. Anna's parents died together, in their car. They were traveling to visit Anna at the school where she received an exceptional education. Anna subsequently integrated the work of Dr. Elisabeth Kübler-Ross into her educational palette and often thought of death and dying. She continues this preoccupation, an aspect of her person that I believe contributes to her great value as a presence in the world. The episode never really ends. Lucille has certainly benefited from the weighted presence of Anna.

I sat at my desk and listened to Lucille's accusations, I considered her inevitable sympathy, her endearing friendship, while fumbling with edge of a document. My intention was to align it with the wood grain of my desk. She said it's good that you have me as a friend. Another man would merely corroborate your action, your infidelity, your deception with the worst possible person. Though maybe she's the best for you, I don't know. I could hear the expression she wore as she spoke, another expression I had seen many times, it was hers alone, something between sensualist and tormented essence.

Though there's nothing of the actress in Lucille. The accents of her face are hers alone, unfeigned. Otherwise, Lucille moves through the world with a lightness of step, good will toward all. But there are a number of males in my life who would likely be critical of what I'm doing, what we're doing, I said. If I told them. Why not share it with them? Her question carried as much pride in being my primary confidante as it did mystification. Because it feels vulgar, the excessive storytelling, the dramatization of my little exploits. You're the only one I really trust outside of my intimate relations. I listened again, to the silence of Lucille. My life is as fully integrated into hers as it can be without our complete physical intimacy. You're a fuck, she said finally. This was followed by an expression of her love for me, and I was happy to have someone in my life with whom I could share such declarations without the compulsion of sex, freighted, erotic thoughts, intervening in that love.

The damage has been done. I'm very clear about this. No amount of analysis will delete what we've done and continue to do because it's life for us, quite far from the death and dying that possesses Anna. My ongoing relationship with Anna's daughter feels like life everlasting. It's neither a midlife nor a late-twenties crisis. It's music, Saint-Saëns, it's a shared aesthetic, a celebration, *Le cygne*. As erotically familiar as it is disruptive of our common qualms about transgression. Of course, an intelligent man or woman recognizes the fact that death is a companion to such music, the old philosophy of death, and that we are always dying. This is one of the many reasons I so cherish Anna. But what we have done to her in life cannot be undone. Ever.

We speed over a country bridge for the sake of speed, we're in no hurry to reach our destination. Bénédicte's hair flies in the wind when she cracks the window, she points out colors and sounds, the cinematic quality of our careening away from the city. One of our occasional getaways, on rare occasions we even leave the country, I am fortunate enough to have a legitimate excuse, my work. Bénédicte only has intermittent contact with her mother, there are few tabs kept between them despite their closeness. Like her brother and father, she could be anywhere at any time. But Bénédicte is different. She doesn't lapse into their turmoil, asocial behavior, she knows what she's doing. She's educated like her mother. She's not a brute. She identifies numerous views from behind the car windshield that take as much of my attention and curiosity as I can afford while driving, the rolling terrain of the countryside, but mostly flat, that expands before us. It eases our senses, the quickly fading greenery. The recent snowfall has melted, it's a little warmer today. It makes us even more amenable to the softer variants of lust shared between us. We speed because it's fun and movie-like.

I cracked my own window, the elation of speed and wind against my face. I leaned out the window, driving. I shouted to the wind—something celebratory, my creed—the things lovers do in moments of inspiration.

And then, how unfortunate, to hit an animal, killing it with our speed. Fast motion rolling over the animal with the car. I stop immediately, we both edge our way over to the creature in the road, there seems to be no suffering beyond the instant of impact. A stray dog. Or more likely, a dog with an owner, a family pet, invariable children who loved the dog. It wears no tags. Bénédicte is profoundly disturbed. I find myself in the mode of take charge, do the best you can with the situation. We sit with the dog for a period of time that feels appropriately sacred. I caress the dog. We retrieve a garbage bag from the car to use as a stretcher and move its carcass to the side of the road, well out of the way of other cars speeding through the country. I get blood on my jeans. There are no houses in the immediate vicinity. Just colors and sounds of the country to which I can now pay closer attention, compelled to do so as I am by virtue of the accident's trigger of intensities, my nerve endings more aware now, our responsibility in this event. It's agonizing to be implicated in violence. The scene resonates with us both, we sit in stillness, huddled around the dog, and observe the day unfolding.

We didn't speak about it as our afternoon progressed. We reverted to driving slowly, there's a pleasure in slow moving that, in fact, surpasses that of speed, this, too, is cinematic. Bénédicte knows what I'm talking about. Feeling the loss and our implication in that loss, rolling through the countryside sights and smells, in the private spaces of our otherwise mingling interiorities, was enough. She kept her head in the car, the window three quarters cracked. Her hair merely danced, a minuet, in the breeze. I wondered how Anna would have reacted to the accident.

Bénédicte sorted through a food basket and we indulged in the meal she had prepared—I love to cook, experiment with food, but couldn't justify this activity to Anna earlier in the morning, before work, fiddling with pastries, packing cheeses, before heading out in a rush—she's done a fantastic job with the food. The countryside gives us everything we've anticipated in the late afternoon, evening is fast approaching, the weather is beautiful. We ate in the car to avoid the remnants of snow, wet ground. Insects went about their day without intervening in our affair. The night at the chateau would afford the usual fulfillment, which is not to trivialize our time together, not at all. There's great beauty in our customs. We get on with the proprietors. They know us and like us, we always share jokes and catch up before retiring to our room that overlooks the courtyard. They know nothing of Anna. The blood almost came out of my jeans with cold water and soap.

In the evening, Bénédicte spoke of her father. Where is he these days? I ask. Anna had not elaborated with me the last time they spoke. He's in Rome, she said, he met someone, a business partner, a new business venture. It's promising but there's pressure. He really needs this to work. Otherwise. I confess to Bénédicte that I sometimes envy the ease with which Ron floats between career developments, all of which seem to work out more or less successfully. I envy him, I do, his freedom. He even manages to evade most of the consequences of his less admirable behavior, with the exception of his marriage to Anna. He was devastated by its collapse. Am I not enough for you? Bénédicte asked straight away, do you really need more than your life offers you? No, I said in answer to her second question. And then, yes, you are more than enough, my joy, my unfathomable, forbidden love, to the first.

In the evening we decide not to have sex, an only slightly awkward non-event. We replaced sex with further conversation, fathers, keeping close to one another, wine. This is the second time that Ron's presence has interrupted a moment of affection with one of his relations and I begin to suspect something cosmic at work, or an additional skill on the part of Ron, in addition to being a successful business man and mature delinquent. Some kind of telepathic kinesis. A supernatural ambush. But really, nothing is upset, my time with Bénédicte in the country, our mutual respect for one another often riding a current between physical and intellectual engagement, our talks often as invigorating as our physical intimacy. We're hardly lacking in emotional expression together. The spiritualism of it all, the psychic warfare fought within the confines of my imagination, I find mostly educational. At one point, we can hear the owners of the chateau exploring the kitchen together.

The morning arrived and with it, a newfound love for one another. It's incredible, the degree to which this thing between us continues to expand into the fabric of our lives, on holiday, at home, at the cinema. She licks my ear, tells a story about Martha Freud, and we have the sex that would have been merely perfunctory last night. I am a master of my life, I think moments after having ejaculated inside of her, holding her close, as she holds me, I can't imagine being anywhere else. We both feel confident in her manner of birth control. But I'll doubtless be even later for work than I had specified to colleagues the day before. There's no need for me to serve her breakfast in bed at the chateau. It's taken care of, in the dining room, by our friends, the proprietors. I've chosen my royal blue turtleneck for today. Bénédicte is fascinated by my getting dressed.

The first time Anna and I discussed marriage would not be the last. Though it set the tone for future discussions. I'm a non-believer in the institution of marriage. How common, how predictable of me, one might think, a man doing what I do, with this person of all people, hanging on to some prehistoric notion of freedom. But it's not a decision I take lightly, I've thought it through. Nor is this to say that I engage in a practice of lambasting those who choose the marriage path. It's just not mine. Lucille, as expected, is mixed about it. She remains unmarried but would ultimately like to find someone other than undersexed academics, or oversexed fetishists, with whom to live, cut vegetables, perhaps marry. It's probably too late for children and she's fine with that, just fine. Anna stares at me for uncomfortable periods of time whenever I explain my position. Tonight she stared harder, and longer, as I turned my usual refrain on the subject of marriage into my own poetry. It contains nothing ugly or vicious—it is, as I put it, a celebration of life, the decision to keep institutionalization at a distance from romantic entanglements. That's a terrible word, she said. We looked it up for the sake of clarity, precision. It's a terrible word. I'm sorry, I said, that's not at all what I meant. Bonds, romantic bonds with others. With a significant other, I added.

Anna stopped me before I could go any further and

suggested we celebrate what we have, now. I've heard about your celebration, I accept it, she said. Let's watch television.

Sitting in front of a television with Anna is very different from the same activity with Bénédicte. With the former, we often land on a drama, a show, a medical drama, the dramatic lives of doctors, patients. I never understand such shows, though when someone's bleeding, the doctors are yelling at one another, lights, dramatic music, the camera closes in on guts, I get that it's easy to be drawn in. But I sometimes find it difficult to sleep after the blood and the excitement. Anna sleeps peacefully. With Bénédicte, it is always film, never a television program. We watch what's on, or she puts in something she's seen many times and wants me to see. We are more often at the cinema than in front of a television. It's a loose analogy, though I sincerely believe that Bénédicte feels about film the way I feel about relations outside the confines of marriage. That they're essential. She and I have never discussed marriage. The mutual but silent acknowledgement of the inappropriateness this topic holds for us.

Of course, Rome is a tremendously demanding city. I've only spent a brief amount of time there, on a few isolated visits, but the speed, the bizarre marriage of the old and the new, the amorphousness of these categories,

I really don't blame Ron for having difficulties there. It's easy to feel overwhelmed amidst the hordes of people, in a speeding taxi, when confronted with the vastness of Rome and the uncertainty of a business matter. One might come to identify with the ghosts of harassed Christians in the coliseum, or with one of the many homeless cats wandering the streets for nourishment, a sense of safety, even someone as hearty as Ron.

As the afternoon wears on, nearing my time to leave, Bénédicte and I raise our glasses, wine, to the health and wellbeing of Ron.

I couldn't remember the name of the client. It completely escaped me as I drove, alone, to my office, the radio on, a window cracked for air. I was thinking of Bénédicte. But what I needed to remember was the name of a client. I had failed to write the name down. Certain colleagues would be tremendously disappointed if I forgot the name at this early stage of negotiations. It would reflect poorly on my attention to detail, a skill that's imperative in my line of work. The radio was playing Hayden, a bit much for the morning, I thought, though I've always heard—folk wisdom, the Mozart effect— that listening to classical music aids one's memory. If this wisdom is true, I thought, then it might be my age creeping in—fifty-something, late fifties, really, forties over, thirties long since vanished—Hayden is doing the best he can to salvage my memory in spite of the aging process. Perhaps I'm getting old, even in this era of extraordinary technological advances, the pervasiveness of yoga, healthier diets.

Or it is simply Bénédicte. I am utterly devoted to her. I'm completely enraptured by this woman who entered my life through the vessel of my partner, whom I got to know incrementally, she was already a young adult. I am so beguiled by my mistress that I'm forgetting essentially trivial information. I don't give a shit about the client. Until the last minute. When the thought of Bénédicte releases me, generously, as it does, to the task at hand. Because she loves me, too, she wants the best for me, and I for her. Negotiations can resume.

Bénédicte introduced me to healthy eating. Another cliché, the younger woman engaging the older man with better ways, healthier approaches, the new, in all of its magnificence. But ours is a relationship that is so much more than the cliché. It is, after all, Bénédicte who champions Saint-Saëns, compelling ideas that branch well beyond the mediocrity of the average twenty-something intellect (late twenties, nearly thirty, I want to be very clear), a groundedness that has a knack for knowing exactly when to take flight and leave the earth, its clients, thoughtless social mores, and when to come back down so that the framework of a life, our lives, is sturdy enough to withstand the transcendence of our being together in the world.

Today she allows me to enter my office without pouring the allness of herself into my thoughts. I walk as a professional today, through the ranks of colleagues, office supplies, expensive furniture outfitting the office that makes clients feel welcome and integrated into the luxury, as if their interests are now in the hands of capable people, a successful firm. It makes them amenable to following through with negotiations. There is a painting here by a celebrated local painter that always arrests the attention of our clients, even those for whom painting is a nothing in their lives, for the artist has contributed to our national identity. I feel a little sickened by this use of nationalism, though it's possible that the former president of the organization, the one who purchased the painting, did so out of a genuine appreciation for modern art. I take my seat at my desk, fumble with something, stare out the window before getting started, so many windows in my life, I think, through which to view the city, the countryside, a generous and captivating woman.

When someone, a colleague, an American, pops his head in my door to say something clever, I'm reminded of a doctor performing a challenging operation on television last night. Horrific, blood spurted everywhere, cinematography that mimics the chaos of an emergency room aflutter. I had asked Anna if this was really something we should be occupying ourselves with before bed and she said yes, yes she enjoys it. I respect this inclination. But I wish I had never seen what I saw on television last night. I was pulled in by a side story of two doctors in the process of dismantling their affair. And a seriously hurt child, with horrible parents. Social services had to be called in. These images work to colonize my thoughts in an instant, though I remain sharp enough, thankfully, to recall the information necessary to the day's work. You must be joking, I say to my colleague.

In the evening, Anna elaborated on a discussion with Ron, also an American, held earlier in the day. She was concerned because he's in Rome—I know, I said, whereupon she looked at me in confusion—and he's had some problems in Italy, in the past. But he's an adult, he's responsible for his own actions, I said. Yes, but the children—yes they are still his *children*, she emphasized the word—it could be hard on them, it is hard on them when he gets into trouble and barely slinks away. They have enough stress as it is, with work, daily life. Bénédicte has been especially distant of late, have you noticed? No, I said. She seems fine to me. And Ron will take care of himself, he always does. Anna stated that perhaps I was jealous of Ron. Hardly, I say. She discerns when I'm not being completely honest.

How did you know his whereabouts? Anna being inquisitive, worried. I don't enjoy seeing her suffer in this way.

But I suspected that the question was filtering its way through the discussion of Ron, Bénédicte, jealousy, and I had been preparing an answer, one that might—would—escape the wisdom of Anna. She called here the other day, you were out, we chatted about this and that, she told me about Ron being in Rome, I said. Why didn't you mention that she called? asked Anna. I forgot, I said. I'm a fuck, I thought.

The season has clearly begun its shift to cool, late autumn, autumn is a flash here, winter will land quickly, as it does. No more picnics for a while. We are faced with an imperative to seize the final days of the season, even in the oncoming chill that has already brought snow. Most of the summer festivals have come and gone. Bénédicte and I saw some very good films, in the afternoons, stood in the presence of a noted actor, a few directors. Bénédicte loathes the theater, so we avoided that, though I am, of course, free to go any time of my own accord, at any point during the year. I don't mind the overextended voices, the props, theatergoers, bows. We experienced some lovely chamber music. But it all adds up, the time away from work, home, the deceit, there is always the danger of seeing friends, acquaintances. Anna, whom I love, in all of her solemn, minimalist beauty, her insights. So we weren't always able to see what we wanted together. Sometimes I took Anna. That's how she views it, still, despite her progressiveness, the social research she does for a living. It's me taking Anna out, regardless of who pays. With Bénédicte, we are merely there, somewhere, together. I've decided that Bénédicte and I should take another trip. She will doubtless agree.

It always feels a bit like teetering on the edge of being prosecuted, planning a trip with Bénédicte. Of being a heartbeat away from arraignment, for some taboo-breaking crime, for some despicable criminality, then committing yet another crime, the new parolee who soon commits a bank robbery. Like Schopenhauer's story of the squirrel, terrified by the presence of a snake in full attack mode, inches away, that moves steadily toward rather than away from the creature that will devour it. Thus identifying with the desire, the ecstasy of the snake more so than his or her—the squirrel's—own survival instinct. Bénédicte tells the Schopenhauer story at dinner parties, I imagine. The obvious problem with the analogy being that Anna is nothing like a snake. I could never live with myself if I ever gave that impression. She is not faultless, she has her eccentricities that needle in the day to day, that limit her being in the world, and by virtue of proximity, our intimate domesticity, my own worldly being. But she is otherwise a model human. She has suffered, thought about suffering, allowed it to inform her happiness. She has no intention of harming anyone, she has a balanced relationship with otherness. Nor is my desire—our desire, I will speak for the both of us, Bénédicte and I—for self-eradication. We share no impulse to be consumed. We are not confused animals, sinners, that's lazy religion, religious drama, something to supplement a lack of thoughtfulness. We merely wish to be happy in our own little way, with as little suffering as possible.

Still, there was an element of walking a dangerous line in making the necessary arrangements for another holiday together.

Bénédicte agreed immediately with the new holiday. We planned our trip for the following month, when the winter weather will be in full throttle. Time in the south, in the sun, sun-bathing together, in between cultural events, holding hands in a Mediterranean city, unconsciously open in our affection, away from the cold. It all came together exceedingly well. I'm eager to be with her in such an atmosphere, without the usual restrictions.

In the meantime, we stroll along Avenue Laurier, not holding hands, it is still a beautiful afternoon, Bénédicte looks wonderful in her sweater and stylish boots. We peer into shop windows and discuss kitchenware, soap. We enter a shop that sells enormous bowls made of candle wax. Anna would like this, I think to myself, and Bénédicte seems to read my thought. She seems to become someone other in that moment, another for whom people tend to mistake her. She comments on the utter lack of utility of an enormous bowl made of candle wax, with a price tag comparable to the object's enormity, its absurdity. I offer to buy her a smaller version, for her bathroom, for when we bathe together, and once again recognize her as my Bénédicte when she agrees, her way of honoring the microscopic shifts and adornments of a lovely afternoon in each other's company. Despite the impertinence of the actress, the aversion to trinkets.

We stop for tea, in a café that caters to the wealthier clientele of this neighborhood, we don't stay long, before traveling east through a section of Parc Lafontaine. The beauty of the open landscape, a body of water around which people gather in the heat of the summer, and occasionally in the colder season, to enjoy the air, the solace of nature amid city life, automobiles. Every such experience is a risk, we know, the chance of being seen and questioned. The risk follows us into the park, everywhere here. The browsing of luxurious household items imbibed with the prospect of implicating us in a crime that surely ranks as sinful in the minds of some. Bénédicte crosses her legs to be more comfortable on the park bench. I cannot help but notice the crease on the backside of her knee, of her skin and the nylon that alters the color of her skin, a dark transparent gray that disappears into her boots, and above, into the folds of her skirt. I can't help it. The degree to which I'm master of my life is curiously dependent on this lack of volition, I think. She comments on the stillness of the water, the lack of people in the park. Before we continue our stroll, it's getting late, nearly time to conclude our afternoon, I remind her that people are generally good.

She interrupts her bath, pushes herself up from the tub of water, aware of the droplets, the sound these make in water, and towels herself before stepping onto the mat. Her new candle bowl is still floating, there's a glowing serenity that is readily apparent in the bathroom, prompted by the dim light, the warm bath water that still undulates quietly in the tub. It's almost a pity to leave the bathroom in such a state. But she can't help feeding her curiosity. She walks uncovered, she will always take a small pride in her body, to the bookcase in the living room, the chill is nearly as nice as the gentle humidity of the bathroom. And there retrieves a book from the shelf, in search of a quote, finds it, reads before slipping back into the water, to continue her bath. She places the book back on the shelf with the others, of which there are many, and ponders the quote once resettled in her bath.

This is how certain people operate. Bénédicte is at once exceptional and spectacularly ordinary.

The following day, Lucille called. She wanted to know if we could meet. We spoke for several minutes, catching up on small developments, little eventualities of our days since having last spoken, she needed to meet in person. Anna overheard our conversation and waved hello, to Lucille, whereupon I interrupted what I was saying—there's a real calmness about a giant bowl made of candle wax, into which one might pour water, float a candle, a kind of monastic beauty—to say hello to Lucille from Anna. The former said hello back, they really do have an affinity beyond the fact of Anna's wise counsel on the matter of death and dying. We agreed to meet for lunch the next day. How is she? Anna asked when she heard me place the phone back in its cradle. Well, I think. She sounds good. Though I have no idea why she wants to see me. There was an urgency in her voice. She wouldn't say. There's often an urgency in her voice, said Anna. Yes, I said. Anna has a way of contradicting me. Or rather, qualifying much of what I say. I'm a little astonished, at work, with Bénédicte, around children, small animals, when I say something that is simply accepted as a legitimate statement, as the closest approximation to truth available to me in that moment. How remarkable, being trusted, indulged. I need more self-confidence. Bénédicte contributes to a newfound confidence but that's not why I'm with her, I'm sharp enough to make such a distinction, at some core of my psychic geography. I'm with her because we resonate together. My trust in her is infinite.

Lucille and I met for lunch. I couldn't imagine what the issue was, or I could, a man, a sibling, disgruntled colleagues, me, my life. She took her time in laying it out. She ordered our food—it's a game, we take turns—asked how are you, Anna, Bénédicte. And as it turned out, the urgency had nothing to do with me, very much to my relief. Lucille is pregnant. A forthcoming child. I knew I had been right in sensing an urgency beyond the usual manner of Lucille. Briefly, I looked forward to telling Anna, a brief preoccupation that didn't conceal an otherwise immediate response to her news. She registered my astonishment despite the fact that I was attempting to be an unruffled presence in her life at that moment, a gift of tranquility, entirely hers in that moment. But it was okay, she had been with this information long enough to remain undaunted by my alarm after the fact. After some man—who is this person, I thought—impregnated her, after a test or a doctor brandished the news. The formula to which I succumbed was to ask, what will you do? Will you keep or abort, the unspoken question. Lucille is in her mid-forties. She spoke.

I don't know. I don't. The pressure, to do that, to bring life. It swells up within me, I feel it, I felt it, rather, earlier, from without, be what you were meant to be, they would imply. I don't know. What if. I'm older, I don't have to spell out the dangers to you, you understand. Or the inconceivable lifestyle shift. It's an impossible thought. But still, I'm not impervious to this biological urge that now has an outlet, me. My child. It's nuts, but. I'll likely die by the time he or she turns thirty, forty, perhaps earlier. That's a lot for someone to handle. We don't need that in our lives. But maybe there's no room for absolutism here, the limited determinacy, the idée fixe of my little mind. My thoughts about what's supposed to happen or not. I don't know. I know that I have a nurturing proclivity. I enjoy the presence of children. I hated whichever of the Disneys that I visited as a child but am fond of word games, hide and go seek, I'm not overly concerned about my body image and am thus amenable to having it stretched, bloated, examined before and after birth. I'm open to this. You know my politics but I'm not keen on eliminating the child unless my life or its life is in danger. Fate. What am I to do with that? My job. Money. You're the first person I've told. I feel ecstatic and afraid. I feel retarded.

My next question: who's the father? You barely know him. You barely met, some months ago, downtown. I know him a little better than I know other people. A colleague. We have a nice time together. We bowled recently. Neither of us enjoyed it very much. We play the lunch/dinner game and generally like what the other chooses, we have that kind of openness—I smiled—there's a nice balance between our mutual pleasures and the gaps in our relating to one another. He's a bit younger, but not too young, that's good—I smiled again, with more obvious pleasure this time—he's got energy, good energy. I haven't told him yet. I see, I said. Our food arrived. It all looked delicious. Lucille asked what I thought.

I'm not fond of eating and talking. There's a naturalness to it, of course, but discussion is best over drinks if one is particularly famished or if one tends to imbue a given meal with metaphysical properties, that approach to food that is worshipful of food. I was neither starving nor personally invested in my meal, delicious though it looked and smelled. This afternoon I was happy to speak to my friend and eat whenever I could, steal moments in between words, ideas, to munch. It doesn't really matter what I said to Lucille. I discussed my own inclinations here. Practical advice. Whimsical suggestions. I was serious. I formulated scenarios. I expressed interest in meeting the father again at some point. The decision was ultimately hers to make and I was confident that the answer was within her. She trusted that statement. Through the menagerie

of schizo-possibilities, fears, ruminations, her everyday
happenings, hers was a metaphysics of affirmation, that
the immaterial becomes material. She trusted that the
answer was within her. She knew it, I think, long before
I spoke. We shared an enlivened hopefulness. She merely
needed me, as I need her, to reinforce the knowable.

When I got home in the evening—I didn't see
Bénédicte in the afternoon—I shared the news with
Anna. She was stunned. There was no need to harp on
the obvious urgency with which Lucille had initially
consulted me.

About Lucille. I often flesh out Lucille to myself.
I think about who she is. A sign of real friendship, it
seems to me, to take the time on occasion to examine
the depth of someone.

She doesn't appear to have aged very much beyond
youth until one sees a photograph, a recent photograph
that stills her movement so that the lines in her face,
the vaguest additions of puffiness to her once aquiline
features, become apparent. I can only speak from the
subjectivity of my own microscopic perspective, but she
remains an image of beauty. On film, in person. Though
it is obviously the personal company of the latter that
I prefer. It should be obvious to anyone who has met
her, the degree to which she operates as a bright spot on
the earth, she magnetizes what is good in life, I would

never joke about her metaphysics. Her eccentricities are equally magnetic, she laughs diabolically when doing something that another might consider faintly obnoxious or intrusive, as a child might laugh when egged on by amused adults. As a child, she was, I have heard, largely within herself, a shy child. And later, as a youth, she emerged into the social with passions developed, securely self-aware, people liked her. Her first serious relationship was with a boy whose parents were modern aristocrats. They met while dancing. They traveled together. His parents liked her. And when it ended, it ended well, on a good note, theirs was a friendship that would last for many years.

She says that her body image is mostly unimportant, a truth relative to her general philosophy of living, though in practice she is healthy, active. People who take especially good care of themselves can afford the luxury of dismissing body obsessions. It's a whole package for her, the interior is reflected on the exterior, her body a temple consecrated to the soul, the substantial taxonomy of what constitutes a soul in her estimation. We've had this discussion for years. And her style, it reflects her age, someone of her distinction, she's not without money, but it's unique without calling excessive attention to itself. She wears tight rather well but looks exquisite in loose-fitting linen, beige, more often than not, that emphasizes her dark hair, cut to her shoulders, a simple cut that could have been styled by an inexpensive barber or a salon professional who caters to the elite, celebrities, noted academics. She eschews the highlights that many women here have painted into their hair. In winter, she wears tight, a black Victorian coat shaped to her body, collar up. When concentrated, she can appear intimidating to men, until they see the softness of Lucille that melts their fears and less admirable sexual inclinations alike. She wears glasses with perfect frames. Her line of work, a progressive occupation.

And then there's the intertwining of our two lives, multiplied, of course, by other relations, stories. Lucille is pregnant. To me she is a triumph of womanhood, which means something very particular to her, the way she does not confuse others with herself, honors what is necessary in her, as spoken by internal rhythms, sage advice from the core. When we first met I was mesmerized by her ingenuity, her good will, the authenticity of her action, assertive, gentle speech, when we met on a project. We worked closely together, I learned from her focus. And then witnessed moments of mild panic, facing deadlines, against the odds, she's human, I thought. She would break the tension by pushing a boundary and laughing at her transgression, without removing her eyes from my own, so that I couldn't help but laugh with her. Our work turned out well. We celebrated, considered intertwining our bodies but found this to be gratuitous in the context of a blossoming, partnering alliance. We had sex but it was less fulfilling than not having sex. Let's stick with being friends, siblings with no blood, fluids shared between us. And then I met Anna.

I watched her draw the curtains from my place on the sofa. We had been there for well over an hour, television, our occasional caresses. I admired her form from that short distance, but more importantly, her characteristic being there, in my presence, for so long, suddenly captivated my attention. I stared at her in quite the opposite way that one stares at a familiar presence and knows, existentially, nothing of that presence despite the years that go into forging its relation. I knew everything about her, as she knew me, everything. With one glaring exception. Or perhaps she knew. The thought of her carrying around this intuition—surely she possessed some disagreeable insight, however obscure, a pinprick in the stern of her thoughts—made me sick in that moment. I excused myself abruptly and went to the bathroom. I heaved a little before the mirror, the sink, the possibility of surprise tears, vomit. Neither of these appeared. Anna knocked and asked if I was okay, her concern all the more catastrophic in that moment. I opened the door, said pointedly that I shall not be watching another medical drama anytime soon. Then I'll refuse to tell you what happens to the child, she said mischievously. Anna could be mischievous. I had no retort. I felt that my life was over. I urged her to be compassionate.

Bénédicte's favorite film, it might surprise some people, is not what one would guess. An Antonioni. A Bergman, Varda. Or more recently, a von Trier, women enduring the most excruciatingly difficult trials. It's quite far from these, though she has only the utmost admiration for such directors, and even our own Arcand. But Arcand doesn't do adults in personal and cultural crisis quite like *The Big Chill*. A fine ensemble cast of American actors, some of whom were not particularly well-known when the film was made. People questioning what it means to be a responsible adult. To be married. A desiring creature in a culture of cardboard marriages. Along with those rare models of liberated matrimony, sharing one's beloved for the sake of another's conception, for example. Tremendously bold. Bénédicte sees herself as being close to that point in life when questions of commitment and libidinal spontaneity exert a certain pressure. She even resembles one of the actresses, her dark hair, slim figure. But this actress is not the one for whom Bénédicte is often mistaken. As for us, our commitment has its own built-in limitations. But I share her appreciation for the film. I once considered snorting cocaine.

When I share Lucille's news with Bénédicte, she becomes quiet. I can't read her, I can't tell if her silence is in honor of this wonder that has befallen Lucille, or if it's a distant reflection on the fact of her own perhaps inevitable childlessness. Like marriage, parenthood is outside the range of acceptable topics for us. Bénédicte still has time to explore this arena of life, but me, me, it's a ludicrous thought, at my age, I can't imagine. Of course, the prospect of her being with another man, a potential father, a younger man, no doubt, *in potentia*, the thought is a little difficult for me. I can only relax and enjoy our pleasure before something like this imposes itself upon us, if indeed this other, a man, a potential child yearning to become in the world, entices her away from me. I think that Bénédicte is like her mother with regards to the processes and creations of her body, her trajectory in and through life. She is very close to her nature, whatever that is. She knows the difference between the natural order of herself and the corporeal and psychic infestation of social flora. She becomes increasingly close to knowing what is right for her. She gets on well with Lucille, naturally, wants only the best for her, but is likely pondering the course of her own life when I share the news about Lucille. I choose to read her in this way when her distance becomes unsettling for me.

I am not a jealous man. I've had moments of jealousy. Terrible, ridiculous moments of a swollen head, puffy with imagination. My partners were not amused. They thought less of me, in fact, and told me as much. Some have been more or less forgiving. I think they all found not a little flattery in the episode, despite their protests. Until one woman was in fact being unfaithful. She was neither flattered nor amused. Strangely, my response wasn't as extreme as when I had merely imagined the infidelity. This led to all sorts of insights regarding the nature of jealously, trust, the possession of people, etc. Now I might imagine Bénédicte with a younger man, feel the sting of that, and then assume the position of the stoic, the even-keeled ship, alone at sea. But cognizant of the sea, its vastness, its fauna, and my own animal nature that is profoundly implicated in the mise-en-scène of the seascape. Bénédicte likes to apply this term from the theater, which she loathes, and film, to physical and psychological landscapes of the everyday. I've long since given up on being jealous where Anna is concerned. The difference between adoration and covetousness.

The next day, Anna and Bénédicte spent the afternoon together. I was a little jealous. Mother and daughter. I wanted to be between sheets with Bénédicte, on the floor, standing in an elevator, our lovemaking generally takes place in a comfortable bed. They were likely discussing Lucille and pregnancy. I don't blame them. How could one avoid the topic of a dear friend contemplating birth? Mother and child, ethics. As I understand it, they had lunch and went to Bénédicte's apartment for tea and further conversation. They are two tremendously bright individuals, I'm certain that their discussion extended beyond pregnancy. Which is not to say that pregnancy is undeserving of an extended discussion. They drank tea, Bénédicte probably put on some nice music, instrumental music, she is wary of vocalists and has nearly instilled a comparable aversion in me, a family afternoon. Her apartment is somewhere between the relaxed comfort of a young professional and the precise minimalism of her mother's aesthetic taste. The home I share with Anna is very much the latter. I like it, we like it.

Anna's bladder has changed since we first became acquainted. This development we also share. Tea and alcohol are especially potent in terms of compelling her to visit the bathroom every fifteen to twenty minutes. Anna apparently did just this at her daughter's apartment. At first, I imagine, she sits quietly, allowing herself to be swayed by the pleasant music on the other side of the door, undaunted by the moment we all encounter, by the solitude that is mandated by excretion, her skirt pulled up around her waist, her staring into a nothingness, etc. But Anna also seeks to fill the space of that solitude, she surveys the accoutrements of the bathroom, its towels, their colors, soap, pictures on the wall, only one of which is erotically themed, the paint job with which I had helped Bénédicte when she first moved in. Anna had contributed other talents to the apartment, sat thinking while we painted, daughter and mother's common law partner. But the object that catches her attention, that continues to absorb her during multiple visits to the bathroom, is the small wax bowl. Perfect for filling with water and placing a candle in its pool to float, move, create ever-changing shadows. Each bathroom excursion sees the music and the other items fade into the unconscious background of Anna's operation there, in that relatively tight space, she fixates on the wax bowl. She is no longer particularly careful to mind the cleanliness of her skirt on the toilet seat. She finally asks Bénédicte about it, comments on how pretty it is, asks where she got it.

It's difficult to say whether or not Bénédicte is an effective liar. She was so earnest as a young adult, before the actress entered her life, our lives. I've only suspected once, twice, and never confirmed that what she was telling me was untrue. It has made little difference, under the circumstances. It makes all the difference to Anna.

When she returned home for the evening, I could sense not that there was a problem, but that Anna had spent time with the woman who has contributed so much to both of our lives. She seemed happy, buoyant. Bénédicte can have that effect. My work went well today, she said. I saw Bénédicte. How is she? I asked. Let's talk, she said.

She wanted to discuss the wax bowl. She remembered my having spoken of it on the phone to Lucille, earlier, before the pregnancy news captivated us. For Anna, the urgency inherent to a tone of voice, another's, had become her own with respect to a bowl made of candle wax, in which one might set a candle afloat for atmosphere, muted light, in a bathroom, for example. She was curious, she saw one of these in Bénédicte's apartment today, not the kind of thing that she would purchase for herself. Do you know anything about this? Did you give that to her?

I hate lying, lies. And they're beginning to add up, I hate this fact about myself. Nor was I privy to Bénédicte's explanation. So I told the truth. I did buy it for her. You saw it? Has she used it yet? I asked. I just thought, after having spoken with her on the phone recently, she seemed preoccupied, perhaps a little stressed, I thought to give her something to lift her spirits. I honestly didn't know if it was something she would appreciate so I'm glad to hear that she's making use of it, or at least displaying it. Where is she keeping it? How does it look?

When did you see her to give it to her? Anna asked. Oh I don't remember, a couple of weeks ago, I suppose.

We met for tea. You met and didn't mention it to me? It was very brief, it didn't seem to warrant mentioning. Anna became quiet. I looked at her as if to question what the problem was, or to act as if there was no problem, I couldn't tell which, I was largely unconscious given the circumstance of having to lie, again. Finally—finally— she moved out of her thoughts, or so it seemed, picked a book off the shelf, as if to continue the work that had gone so well during the day. She said nothing more about the wax bowl. And I had the sense to do the same. I entered my own study, we each have one, funded, in part, by the divorce support of Ron. He hates that Anna and I remain unmarried. We spoke no more about it.

Later that evening, when Anna was in bed, I made a discreet call to Bénédicte. She wasn't home, leaving me to wonder where she might be, with whom she might be out on the town, dancing, discussing Saint-Saëns. I left a message and was very grateful for mobile phones, tactful messaging, as opposed to the tape machines of my generation, the messages of which could be overheard by a visiting mother. I told her what I told Anna, about the wax bowl. If she asks, I said, you need to be informed. I told her that I love her before concluding the message and hanging up. Bénédicte, as it happened, had also told the truth about the origin of the wax bowl.

I of all people am not unaware of the fact that identifying oneself too keenly with another whom one resembles may be a marker of immaturity. I know because when I was younger, people sometimes commented on my resemblance to a famously handsome politician, it's true. He was always on television, giving interviews, sporting a rare confidence that dazzled his interlocutors, that still dazzled the press, television viewers, after the popularity of his party began to wane. I once saw him wearing leather pants on a casual public outing. And as much as I was disaffected by his politics, I enjoyed the attention. And then, nothing, nothing really happened to shift this experience beyond his fading into bureaucratic history. But when people misrecognized me, I always sensed that trickle of elation and for a brief moment became a representative of everything that is ugly about our culture whose driving force is entertainment. I became an ambassador of the ocular regime, a mere face. And later I would regret this momentary transformation. This descent into politics. As though something central to myself had been lost.

But really, I'm making too much of it. I remain intact. It's just, Bénédicte, I often see her teetering on the edge between her mother—her clear, elegant movement through life, her depth in the valley of the shadow, dying—and her face. As though the music, her intelligence, our shared intimacy, weren't enough for her. They have always been enough for Anna. Bénédicte enjoys the attention. How ironic that she would question whether she is enough to satisfy me. I sometimes wonder what I'm doing with a woman who is nearly half my age and whom many, from the standpoints of both familial logistics and emotional proximity, would consider to be my daughter. And then I remember exactly what I'm doing.

Oh, and to those who might grow weary under the weight of my ongoing self-recriminations, do recall our mutual humanity. It will help. Take a moment to feel the air we share in your lungs, breathe deeply. Think of nature. Or, alternatively, just go to hell.

At the theater, Anna and I rush to our seats just before curtain. The lights dim, we barely have time to peruse our programs, look at bios, credits, advertisements for diamond companies. I can sense the brains of the production kicking into gear all around us, an anxious stage manager in the booth behind us, music, lights, actors gearing up for a performance. They do what they can to make it look seamless, and it often is, but one perceives the nervous energy, people taking deep breaths behind the scenes, voice exercises, gearing up to act. You're a giraffe, a wounded giraffe, feel that hurt, voice it, through the cylinder of your extended neck, emote, elongate. A director biting his nails. I, too, am beginning to loathe the theater. But Anna is excited, and I do enjoy the anticipation of the oncoming spectacle, not knowing what's going to happen. Who wouldn't? And then the actor appears, the first of a noted ensemble cast, she looks forlorn there before us, she manifests sorrow, rumination, as well as anyone I have ever seen onstage. She will soon be joined by the others, a drama played out before us as though simply emerging from life, rather than from months of laborious and typically melodramatic rehearsals.

Act two, I'm bored. But the sets are good. We do those well here, in this city. I catch Anna mouthing some of the lines. She knows the play, she has a good memory for these things, though I'm still surprised by the poetry. She appears to be having a wonderful time, I enjoy the lightness of our being together here, the quality of our time together often determined by the state of Anna. Barring the sets, some solid acting, it all strikes me as too unreal, futile, funereal. Why bother? I ask myself. I'm getting closer to agreeing with Bénédicte, that the theater is a dying animal. Acting, something most of us do without training, rehearsals. We choose not to get up and join the rest of the audience in the bathroom, for wine during intermission. It's not a long play. It seems we will both hold out on the bathroom despite our bladders. Anna and I haven't had much opportunity to talk today, so we talk in our seats at intermission. She tells me about a new face cream, and then a book. I speak about health, the pinching of my new shoes. When the lights go down again, we've covered a fair amount of territory. Anna places her hand on my knee and braces herself for the climax.

It comes like a torrent. A wind machine howling, screaming actors. Dialogue being spat out, violence with words, set furniture. Incredible the degree to which they demolish the set and then rebuild for the next performance. Theater tricks. I once got blood on my pants from sitting on the front row. Some sort of syrup concoction, as the apologetic stage manager put it to me afterwards. The theater covered the dry cleaning bill. The stage manager had attempted to wash the blood out herself, in the men's bathroom, but it remained despite her efforts, down on the floor, scrubbing my pants with cold water and soap, her face in my crotch, a performance of sorts that continued after the performance, very erotic. Tonight, just yelling, stage violence. Anna has stopped mouthing the words, she sits, enraptured, though clear in herself, she will assure me after the play, that such drama need merely be an occasional exercise, on the stage, away from the solace of our home. It's not really to her liking, riveting though it can be. It is not essential in the architecture of a life. We have a late night dinner, what feels like a late night Manhattan dinner, after the play, where we discuss drama over a very delicious meal. The relative quietude of the restaurant is a balm for me.

Many have commented on the distinct pleasure of going to the cinema in the afternoon. From lightness to dark, and back to light. The light is different from what it was before you entered. You notice your feet differently as they carry you to the car after the film, the metro, a corner for a taxi, or if you're fortunate enough to live close to a cinema, home.

Bénédicte and I walked to the car, we enjoy driving together, the stillness of the confined space, our control of music. Sometimes, as on this day, we park, on the mountain, a secluded space that overlooks the city or wedges us into the forest where no one pays us any attention. Where we—two professionals—join in the mechanics of nature and fondle one another among leaves, self-defeating squirrels, overhanging rocks.

We walked in silence. Our time after the film echoed the silence of the film, talking would have been sacrilegious. Until we got in the car and looked at one another, still silent, our expressions making the same gestures, asking the same questions about the film, wondering, if it is really necessary, if we really have to emerge from this place to which the film had transported us. There, there was the sole violence of the film, there it was, the mandatory entering back into the world of a city, lives, familiar streets, suspicions on every corner. I made a funny face at Bénédicte. She didn't want to give in to the levity of my new expression, she wanted to bask in the seriousness of the film, but she finally gave in when I persisted, contracted my face even further, something hideous, she did the same—professionals, the two of us, in the car, making faces—and then we began to talk about the film.

How does one engage with something like that? There's the obviousness of sitting still, not talking, don't eat popcorn at a film like this, it's loud, unhealthy. Being awake, attentive to as much of the filmic world as possible, its movement, sound, the exceptionality of its time. Moments of pulling back from the film, feeling oneself, one's body, in a theater with other bodies, other modes of attention concentrating, the differing levels of self-awareness in the dark. The exceptional play of light in the space of the theater. But a film like this, it requires more. It invites you to be superhuman. Even as you identify and dis-identify with characters, events, that rolling process of heightened spectatorship, as when one watches a catastrophe on television, in real time, or just after, it doesn't really matter, the effect is the same. Immense viewing. The invitation of the film is to unfurl, and to view oneself unfurling in perfect alignment with it. To be and to become with the film.

Bénédicte cried at one point. It had been a very long

time, years, since I myself had felt moved at the cinema to that degree, speechless. And not as a consequence of puerile emotions, triggers, but by silent, nuanced acting, followed by a camera, a well-placed microphone. The dialogue that hits nails perfectly into the solid wall without cracking paint or sheetrock. Without saying too much. With very little music, what's there hits perfectly, more sounds than music, emphasizing the crevices of acting, filling in gaps, or not, sounding silence between acting words.

And as for the conclusion. They did what needed to be done, the characters with whom Bénédicte and I resonated, there, in the theater. The one, fading after this final, monumental act of touching another was accomplished, he faded into the darkness, outside the couple's room once the contact had been made, an erotic moment shared between them, he closed the door behind him. While the other, she moved closer into foreground, she, as slow as only she could have been after that devastation, that awful pleasure of being touched. Her face, the authenticity of her face, a look of ruin, gratification, intelligent defeat. And our mutual reflection there in the wake of something quiet and serious having obliterated our pasts and turned the future into snow, at the cinema.

We felt the initial chill of the unheated car, the two of us sitting there while the car warmed up. I always have mixed feelings about the coming of winter. It was good not to have to walk far today. And then I made a face at Bénédicte, whereupon she struggled to stay in the film, to remain forever, one might imagine, in the room that zeroed to that point of extreme darkness. The characters, the final scene, the room all fading into nothing, not quite the light beam of pure white transcendence, but close, our comfort and desolation in the dark blurring with those of the actress. And then she gave in, Bénédicte, she did something terrible with her face, we laughed, I did something worse with mine. And then it was okay to discuss what we had just experienced at the cinema, on our way to her apartment, to drop her off. It was nearly evening, time, back to the consequential life of clocks.

TWO

Mine is a lumbering shadow.

I don't feel that it represents me at all. It's embarrassing, in fact, to see that thing in front of me, grounded before me. It's all out of proportion, the too small head, the pear shape, the fruitiness of its contours. The arms extend in such a way as to appear stretched, and bent at the wrong place, the product of Gothic fiction. The entire flat, dark lumbering image belies the work I do, still, to keep my body fit, as it has generally been throughout the duration of my young and adult life, middle-age. An unfortunate byproduct of walking in the sun, under a street lamp at night. It must be a lie. And yet, when I'm with another, Bénédicte, Anna, or a friend, still pregnant, still deciding, I find the other's shadow to be perfectly congruent with the physical presence walking beside me. Everything matches up just fine. Which suggests that I do in fact resemble my shadow. A graceless thought. That the mirror image I see every day, in the morning, trips to the bathroom to relieve my bladder, or at night, brushing, flossing, is not the real me. It is, rather, this gauche silhouette that people see, address in different ways according to the nature of our exchange, Good morning, Monsieur, Get the fuck out of my way, cretin, Ma cheri, My love. Such a thought to give one pause when, as Anna reminds me periodically—our discussions of her work, her coming to terms with life—death encroaches upon every little *now* constituting the time of our days, decades, our every little milieu. I'm a monster.

Bénédicte's tears, which I rarely see, have a profound effect on me. I myself haven't really cried in years. Likely due to the socialization of men, particularly those of my generation, my age—it's been ages since I had good hair to comb, style, flail about—though men in general, I think, are not really allowed this activity except in the most dire of circumstances, terrorism, natural disasters. The last time I cried was when a sibling died. Death. The natural disaster of losing a loved one. Nature saying come on let's go, another round, if you want to look at it that way. We weren't especially close. But the sadness of it all, the whole affair, was daunting. The initial impact was followed by a celebration of life, the time of this relatively young life cut short. But a valuable life, validated by emotional attachments, my sibling's life, some accomplishments that have been recorded, will be remembered. There was cake, good food, comforting food. It was lovely to catch up with some of the relatives.

With Bénédicte, the weight of that sadness is absent for me. None of the difficulties through which we've lived—as a clandestine couple, a family unit— have been incomprehensible. We've moved through and on. And yet, there's an eroticism to her tears that would be dishonest of me to deny. My own eroticism, of course, projected and nurtured by an inclination to always remain attuned to her sexual being. Its relation to me, my desire for her, even in tears. We reflect, as a species, on the extent to which sexual instinct pervades the daily life, but we rarely include instincts for sadism, masochism, taboo eroticism, the veiled filth, in our personal inventories of this is all part of the beautiful interesting tapestry that forms my life. Rather, we, most of us, shield ourselves from these undesirable desires. Bénédicte has a lot to say about this matter. So concerning Bénédicte, I take pleasure in her vulnerability. I like seeing her break down, on the rare occasion that this happens—she's a strong individual, focused, easily amused—I take pleasure in witnessing the cavity of her person become filled with whatever it is that moves,

hurts, remembers, fears, all that figures into the domain
of an actress persona but is, in fact, very real indeed in a
given moment of tears. Those moments when I console,
do what is necessary to be an anchored presence,
and then want her with great ferocity. We've had one
another under such circumstances. It was exceedingly
memorable. But certainly, certainly, her needs come
before my own. This, too, is part of my psycho-sexual
make-up. I am as much a caring lover, a compassionate
man, as I am what one of Anna's poems might refer to
as a libertine. I don't remember the last time I witnessed
Anna cry. I honestly don't.

The first tragedy of the day was the event of having
mistakenly dirtied a smaller rather than a larger spoon
to aid in the process of blending fruit for breakfast. It
meant either stretching my hand into the blender further
than it really needed to go, thus risking mixed fruit all
over my hand (a wash, a towel off, further actions to
slow the morning's prep), or placing the already spoiled
small spoon into the sink where it would be yet another
dish to wash and replacing it with the larger spoon. We
don't have a dishwasher. It's not that we can't afford one.
We could afford several. But I don't like them. Their
noise, an action that I can perform just as easily without
the clamor of machine washing and rinsing. But I'm not
always very fond of hand washing either. It's especially

frustrating in the morning, before work, in the event
that the dishes weren't done the previous evening. I
finally brought out a larger spoon. It'll be a fast wash,
both of them at once. I can handle it. In retrospect, it
isn't a tragedy per se. But in the moment. The way we
are sometimes. Still, the blended fruit mix, though a
little spoiled by the extra washing, was delectable. I was
glad to endure this process alone, before Anna made
her way to the kitchen, her own isolated preparations
forthcoming.

Little things going wrong, etching into the canvas
of the day. And then, later, the awkward shuffling on
the sidewalk, in front of people, colleagues, an ordinary
walking pace interrupted by the shuffle of a foot, its
scraping the ground, the hard sole of my shoe failing
to lift—it's a simple procedure, I do it all the time,
walking—and instead abrading the cement of the
sidewalk. Some trouble with walking. It was a cloudy
day, I am thankful for not being witness to my ungainly
shadow. A movement that set the tone for the rest of
the walking conversation with colleagues who surely
noticed my misstep, that sound I made with my foot.
He's an imbecile, they think. Me, I can't even walk.
Such thoughts that don't provide one with a firm basis
in holding one's own, discussing weighty matters in the
company of professionals.

There were others in the conference room

meandering, later, awaiting my presentation when I entered. I have an aversion to many electronic devices—I've witnessed their magic, I applaud these innovations, but don't trust them when one's project, or an impetuous holiday, is on the line—so I prepared charts with a magic marker. Anna had watched as I made them the night before and reached a level of mirth that I haven't beheld in her in some time. The others finally sat down around the conference table, they continued to chat until I stood in silence at the head of the table, placed one hand in the other and waited patiently. A man prepared. I cleared my throat. I spoke eloquently. My project was sound. I carried my listeners. I hit that moment during the presentation when I knew instinctively that I had them. My charts were a success, perhaps due in part to their simplicity, their innocence, people felt relaxed around the childlike clarity of my charts. They were mesmerized, that is precisely the word I used to myself in the back of my mind and between the eloquent words that issued from my mouth with increasing comfort. The graciousness of my person, my worth to the organization, was apparent to them. Why not just use a computer, one of the others said when I was done.

Bénédicte is unable to meet this afternoon.

In the evening, Anna and I decided to make a squash risotto. Not a difficult meal. Quite easy, in fact. Butternut squash, orange peel (grated), parmesan sprinkles, parsley, white wine, broth, risotto rice, lots of stirring. The only real difficulty lies in removing the outer layer of the squash and cutting the squash in bite-sized pieces. Always my job, I use a peeler, and then a large knife. I didn't cut myself, thankfully. The object is to fill a whopping two cups of bite-sized pieces, a simple enough task, until I'm informed that, no, smaller, they must be smaller, they'll cook quicker. Of course they will. We've been through this many times, Anna and I. This particular evening, I had done a marvelous job with the cutting. And just before the squash is to enter the pot, she comes behind me, picks up the knife, and proceeds to cut the pieces smaller. I stand in the background of the kitchen, there's nothing more for me to do, I watch Anna correct my work. I'm ill-suited to anything outside of pleasuring your daughter, I said, or wanted to say, but merely thought to myself. Perhaps next time I'll purée the squash, I said. I said this. Anna did not find the humor in my comment because there was none. With locally made maple syrup and a little salt from the Himalayan mountains, the risotto was not a disappointment.

To bed. To the end of a long day. I would dream of the country. Of the dog I killed and its potential family of dog owners, their immense hurt, sadness. And then of a previous relation, enacted by others in the dream who clearly represented the two of us, myself and a former love, our relative youth and its pleasures. The plague of the day dissipated along with its last waking moments. Anna fell asleep quickly. In the country, in the dream, a fresh beginning, smaller, less adulterated creatures than myself living and breeding.

Bénédicte called on my mobile phone. I have one of those. She wants me to get one with a camera but I refuse, entirely too much to think about, too many options, pictures and talking, in a variety of modes. She said that she wanted to talk, hear my voice. I could tell that putting work aside for a moment, stealing away with her in my office, her voice, the gentleness of her tone, was exactly the right thing to do in this moment. She wanted to discuss anything. And later, specifically, the film she saw the previous night, the bath she had, my wardrobe. No one could see me in my office with the possible exception of someone in an equally tall building with binoculars, across the way. It was unlikely. Had someone seen me, however, I would have appeared as a proud father. I don't mean the father of Bénédicte, no not that at all, just a father, the way such a person is when he recognizes the intimacy of a loved one, someone younger, the inimitability of that one, how integral he or she is to his life, this unique other informing male existence. A defining moment. That Bénédicte resembles an actress is mere circumstance.

The afternoon was spacious, easy, the light in Bénédicte's apartment touched the white brick walls without fanfare, illuminated without intrusion, the white bed sheets, still rumpled on the bed, a black and white postcard that communicates morning sensuality, Parisian ease, in a way that really fit our mood, the comfort in which we lounged in the afternoon together, in the living room of Bénédicte's apartment. I made tea while Bénédicte looked at a magazine on the sofa. Street noise beyond the windows that one might come to miss in the quiet solitude of the country, but only for a moment. The peace of the country silence enveloping one, supporting one's nobler instincts and aspirations. But how lovely to be in the city today, in this apartment, with Bénédicte, perfect light, she decided to have green tea with me, I hope she'll sleep tonight.

She put on some music, not the usual fare, but an old female jazz vocalist accompanied by the conventional band. I was a little put off at first, surprised by the voice, the only woman I wanted whispering to me was Bénédicte. Until I came to realize the absolute appropriateness of this music as an accompaniment to our afternoon together. Triggering as it invariably did smoldering people gracing a room with the single-pointed concentration of their music, their life's direction. I had purchased the tea on a business trip, to the States, visited an Asian market and bought what was recommended. Bénédicte was very much taken by the green tea and said it was worth it even if she wouldn't sleep well that night. I asked her what her plans for the evening looked like and she made a zero sign with her hand. I felt a little reassurance in this. Picturing her in front of a film, or holding a novel, her highly valued solitude. Perhaps reflecting on the pleasure of our time together. Having a solitary walk, dreaming in the night, on foot.

And yet, there was no way, I thought, that the knock on the door could have signaled anything other than an unwanted incursion into our afternoon together. And though Anna will testify that I am often wrong, about many things, often I am right. This can only be a problem, I thought, and was more or less correct. I thought to hide when Bénédicte moved to answer the door, but somehow this seemed entirely too childish, I'm an adult, I've long been an adult. The last time I hid under such circumstances, the girl's parents would very definitely have underappreciated my presence in their home, in their daughter's bedroom, wearing that outfit. I started to hide and then thought better of it, sat on the sofa. Picked up the magazine, a relaxed man.

It was Ron.

Bénédicte couldn't remember when she last saw him. Two, three years ago. He just showed up, as he likely did last time, two or three years ago. We'd been through this, as a family, many times. I knew the level of turmoil through which this man had put the others, his children, ex-wife. I was aware of how Bénédicte must have been feeling as she moved through her shock at seeing him, and then, surprisingly, her calm, even her affection towards him, their embrace. Ron didn't seem to think twice about my being there. He walked over, shook my hand, smiled the smile of someone who has been living a large life in Rome, or wherever he happens to be stationed at this juncture. He sat down without being asked to do so. Bénédicte offered him tea but he requested a glass of water instead. Before I could ask the obvious question, what brings you to town, he began to explain his visit, some time between jobs—there was something a little unsettling to me about the word job, its ties to underworld crime, but really, I like Ron, I can't imagine he's become that wayward—he thought to see the family. I had no reason to doubt this, to think that he had an ulterior motive. Excellent, I said. Though he had still interrupted what was shaping up to be a gorgeous afternoon with his daughter. Bénédicte had turned down the music.

I really do like Ron. His surface details, proportions, distinctly American mannerisms, they are all as one might expect after having seen multiple versions of this character on television, in American films, *The Big*

Chill. I suppose the same can be said of many people, from a variety of cultures. I admire Ron's confidence, a little brash, it's true, but honest, forthright. Except when he lies. People might say the same of me. That I am genuine, occasionally heartfelt, except when I stretch or abbreviate or demolish the truth of a matter. Ron's pleasure in being with us, but especially with Bénédicte, seemed genuine.

He told stories of his recent ventures, he held forth in the way that he can. I was amused, Bénédicte was more or less enthralled by the presence of her father, sitting there on her sofa, in front of her. He's a good storyteller, I thought. I wonder if I could beat him at any games, athletic activities. It was the kind of question that I suspect a man of my generation is inclined to ask when faced with another of his own ilk, sitting there strong, confident, before him. I asked him if he missed America and he waved his hand, said no, Rome, Roma, that's my home, and I said I understand. Busyness, scooters, history, cats. Yeah, he said. We discussed Italian cuisine, Fellini. Bénédicte eventually got up to do I'm not sure what, move about the space. She made a call. A brief moment of silence between myself and Ron. He smiled and said I'm surprised to see you here. A sporting event after all, I thought.

Or not really. It was an innocent comment, made from the unaffected simplicity of Ron. But I was placed

in the position of having to make a sport out of it.
Nothing wrong with a mother's partner visiting her
daughter. But there was the statement that wielded a
potential accusation, requiring more, it seemed to me,
than a mere, I just stopped in to say hello, like yourself,
only I'm not living six thousand miles away. We are,
after all, family. The way communication is these days,
you know, a kind of messaging that merely resembles
communication, it's healthy to stay in touch, a family
visit, nothing more. But I settled on a quick excuse. A lie.
I dropped by to pick up a book, I said. Ah, which book?
he asked. Whether or not he was genuinely interested in
which book, Ron was winning the match, or the game,
whatever it was. I wanted to think of it as a tennis match.
Me, the elegant Swede, Bjorn Borg, naturally, him, the
irascible McEnroe (our early adult years in the 1970's).
My serve. The umpire had to tell someone in the stands
to be quiet, please.

Thoughts racing to remember Bénédicte's bookcase,
which I couldn't scan, it would have been too obvious.
And finally. A book of her choosing, I said triumphantly.
A novel to read at night. You know Anna's proclivity for
reading at night. I've decided that this is the point in my
life where I, too, should begin to take literature seriously.
Expand my thoughts. Live vicariously. Not all of us have
your penchant for real life adventure—Ron smiled at
this—so I'll content myself with joining characters on

the printed page. I knew Bénédicte would get me off to an excellent start. Look at all those books there. I pointed to the bookcase. I still don't know what she's going to choose for me but I'm ready to be her pupil. This last line was perhaps a bit excessive but Ron smiled again, still quietly pulsing over my compliment, it seemed. I threw my racket in the air, ran and jumped the net. Not as the obvious victor—there was no need for this, my victory was far too nuanced, too subtle to be celebrated in that grand way of championship matches—but as a cheerful and worthy opponent. Shared a few words with Ron, my arm across his shoulder, before gazing triumphantly into the stands, the cheering crowd. Such was the way of my miniature battles, my curious manhood.

When Bénédicte completed her phone call—to whom could she have possibly been speaking?—I stood and reminded her of the reason for my visit. So which one is it going to be? Where shall we begin? She didn't move from where she was leaning against a mantle. But Bénédicte is sharp. She eventually walked over to the books, taking her time, as though really weighing the choice. She chose a collected poems by a Czech poet. A poet, not a prose writer. Bénédicte. But it didn't seem to make any difference to Ron, who was clearly looking forward to some time alone with his daughter. I had been enjoying the same until he arrived. I shook hands with Ron. It really was nice to see him. He looked well.

Bénédicte and I hugged. Quite disingenuously, it felt to me, relative to the act of embracing one another on an ordinary afternoon, following the hours of our time alone, enveloped by white sheets, light.

It occurred to me, on my way home to Anna, a bit earlier than one would have expected, to wonder what Ron would think, or do, if he found out. Ron, too, is a libertine, though of a distinctly different variety from myself. I'm inclined to say that he lacks the poetry of my existence (I know, I know…) but makes up for this lack with bravura. Me, I'm a secret (mostly), a hidden jewel, a quiet tomb containing riches. Ron is open, not a little crass, relates his escapades in the manner of conventional narrative. You should have been there, and then, you won't believe this, etc., etc. But she's his daughter. Men watch out for their daughters. They seek revenge. But perhaps he would understand. I won the match, I can hold my own with Ron. I felt a little sick at having my time with Bénédicte cut short.

I once accompanied a friend to have his driver's license renewed in New York. It was there, at the Department of Motor Vehicles, that I came to know America. Its speed. Its polite capitulation to the Law, tempered by an occasional resolve to be obstinate, to be vocal in one's obstinacy. New York politeness, or its inverse, is a mere shade of the larger American sensibility, but people were generally friendly, joking, a general air of lightness in the otherwise bureaucratic domain of sign tests, photography, waiting. I witnessed strangers joke to one another, their smiles. Laughs about their hair in the photos. All kinds of people in and out. A melting pot. What a dumb phrase. Let's be more accurate, I thought: a people with distinct borders, hopelessly conservative tendencies. Of course, the people in my part of the world, just over the border, have no compulsion to erect further borders. No, they don't have that compulsion. No, not at all (Separatists ...). But my friend made it out of the DMV with surprising speed, a handsome photograph, good hair. Clear to drive. To speed when the cops are attending to other, more deleterious crimes. A slice of America. Rugged people. The entertainers of the world, infinite possibilities.

Bénédicte is half American. It's in her blood, as they say. She used to spend summers there, again, in New York. I love this about her. I don't need to romanticize, I'm long since over romanticizing people, places, but it seems an ideal combination, the possibilities of her American blood, that unique energy, and becoming blood sister to her people of the north, francophone energy, literacy, Europe. Anna was quite young when she gave birth to Bénédicte. She once told me that the night Bénédicte was conceived, there was blood. Bénédicte born of a harrowing, bloody first experience. A blood nexus between two cultures, the concentrated, elegant Anna, and Ron.

Camille Saint-Saëns was not an attractive man. Unlike his good friend Liszt. A brilliant and technically proficient musician and composer, of course. But he was large, a poorly sculpted nose, bloated cheeks, especially in old age. His *Symphony No. 3* is magnificent, as are some of the later, slightly more experimental chamber works. Looks were not as important to the musician as they have become in the age of television, film, actors in advertisements. Another interesting fact: he went under the name of Sannois for a spell, his efforts to escape a politically torn Paris, to live simply, I like to imagine. The kind of name that invites a quality of ease. But what is perhaps most interesting about Saint-Saëns is that he was one of many in the audience who witnessed, and walked out on, the premiere of Stravinsky's *The Rite of Spring*. From the vantage point of contemporary music appreciation, this seems absurd. But that's how people are. Quick to disapprove of, or to flea from what doesn't immediately fit into the purview of codes, musical or otherwise. People rioting over a musical performance, a ballet. I like to imagine Saint-Saëns eventually regretting the decision to walk out on the infamous concert. I remain stringent in my conviction that we are all basically good.

The note on Anna's desk that I read this morning—
it was nothing for me to glance over her things, we do
it all the time, we have that kind of openness, though
my desk is messier than hers, less inviting of perusal—
was indecipherable. I could read it, I did read it, but it
was suddenly difficult to understand the contents of
this note, a "thank you for yesterday," followed by an
"I know you will shine, the stage is your home, you
have answered, you'll be great." I could not begin to
comprehend what this was about, its implications, the
secrecy of it all. I had no idea who had written such a
note, what had happened yesterday, the mystery of Anna
performing, in front of people. It was signed, merely, L.

I contemplated asking her about it. And then, no, no
I'll await her explanation. She'll tell me if it's important.
She tells me everything. And if not, if the note and its
would-be significance vanish with no account, I'll leave
her to her secret. Secrets. She deserves them. I'm not
a jealous man. Though I have perhaps strengthened
the drama of death in a woman whose life is so fully
integrated into my own.

Bénédicte appreciates the fact that I rarely wear
ties. I hate them. It's more in keeping with me to wear
an open-necked oxford—but not too open, I should
clarify—and blazer. Very likely a sweater in the colder
months, which feel like many here. A sweater with a

six-inch zipper, give or take, and a collar that stands up around my neck, flapping on its side just at the brim, a little lazy, casual. I'm a little lazy, fussy only when pushed, perhaps an anomaly in this particular culture of men, their Catholicism. Anna once suggested I buy some dress loafers and I said yes, for an unfathomable amount of money, I'll wear those in public. That's not the kind of casual I prefer, it's not at all my style. A small point of tension with Anna.

Bénédicte says to me, on the phone, I love that you are not a boring merde the way you dress, there's still an edgy young man in there, in the body of your middle age. You don't go too far in the other direction either. No call for that. Desperate hankering for youth. You are elegant, like maman. You look good in the right pair of jeans, still. Men can be fortunate that way. However. Bénédicte offers small additions to my wardrobe, occasionally purchasing something for me, a surprise in the afternoon. Your underwear are grotesque. I've gotten some new ones for you. And the color in your sweaters, it sometimes goes a little far, like the other men here, the slightest remnant of tie-dye, please don't. It's defeatist of you. Your darker colors are fine. I bought you something today. She loves outfitting me in clothes that are just on the edge of being too tight. I do work out, after all. The dark gray of the new shirt matches your eyes, she says. I love her even when I hear her mother speak through her, telling me, in her joyous way, that I am incomplete.

She had wanted to go away together for some time, so we did. To New York. We bounded out of our own beloved city, by taxi, plane, and landed just outside the city, more taxis, check in, everyone very polite, asking about our accents. We love New York. It's so close. And yet another country entirely. A separate galaxy. It's been cleaned up over the years, gentrified, for better or for worse. We stayed in Tribeca. A perfect location from which to begin a long walk in the morning, to take in the city in all of its largeness. Upon arrival, we stopped by a small market to get a few items for the room, perhaps to remind ourselves of our home and its own relative size. Or simply to eat when the mood strikes.

The hotel rooms are all just off circular corridors, opening onto circular balconies that overlook the first floor, its check-in area, lounge and popular bar. A lovely arrangement until one attempts to sleep. Anna was not pleased. Until we realized that there was a sound device just above the door to our room. A sound generator, white noise that would issue from a speaker and mask the late night noise from the bar. This worked more or less. I suggested we install one of these to mask the occasional sound of snow plows on our street at home. She liked the idea, though I was only half serious. Little things we can do to make our life together more convenient.

In the morning we began a walk, through neighborhoods with great character, stopped at galleries, boutiques, had tea, observed people. I picked up a paper and we discussed various possibilities for the afternoon and evening, and for the following day, it was to be a short trip, for the long weekend. Our culture practices innumerable holidays. There was a play that Anna wanted to see. I was mostly interested in walking, seeing, listening, employing all of the senses, really. The grittiness that accumulates upon and around one after walking the city streets for an extended period of time, the way it feels in one's hair and clothes. We took the metro to the park, for the experience of taking the metro there. It's different from our own system, more skeletal, graffiti. Where we encountered young, nouveaux punks, very friendly, and a man who had just purchased a pornography DVD that he displayed without thought, the title and cover of which pertained to anal sex. Anna and I laughed quietly to ourselves until he began to light something on the train, something other than a cigarette, the flame was greater than one would expect to encounter on the metro, and we decided to get off at the next stop. It really wasn't that much further, the park. Stepping out into the clear light of day, a cold walk, though nothing we weren't used to. The day was warming as we walked. I held Anna's hand. I motioned for her to—look—and pointed to a man selling chocolate-covered strawberries on the street.

I've come to have doubts about the theater. People in costumes, yelling. There was a strong erotic content to our evening's play that cut down on the use of costumes, even the yelling, much of it was surprisingly quiet. Most of the gasps and moans came from the audience. Quite far off Broadway, it felt, though it's still fascinating the degree to which we wince at eroticism, particularly live acts of eroticism. I wanted to discuss this with Anna in the middle of the play, which began to feel tedious, there was no intermission, but our voices would have hindered the erotic flow. At one point a paranoid protagonist, in fear of authoritarian tinkering with his life, his free thoughts, stuck his fingers into the panties of his female guest in order to explore her sex for a recording device. This action marked the height of the audience's auditory response and I myself reacted as much to the audience as to the onstage fingering by a noted actor. We waited until dinner to discuss the play, a late night New York city dinner that was even better than the ones we often share in our home city six hours north.

That Anna had discussed the book of Czech poetry with Bénédicte, many months prior, and found the book among my things just before our departure—there was no possibility of questioning the fact that she had been going through my things, we are generally open, there was no call for that given what she had found, and later, heard—was reason enough for her suspicions to be raised (an innocent enough discovery, really, I enjoy books, as many thoughtful people do). But as it happened, Ron was more insightful, or attentive, or competitive, than I had given him credit for. Or perhaps he was merely making small talk when he mentioned to Anna that I was with Bénédicte at her apartment when he dropped by unexpectedly. This fact raised Anna's suspicions to another level, a level previously unknown to her. For she is not a jealous person—better even than I—and I've never given her reason to be jealous beyond a head turn on occasion, in public, or a mild comment expressing pleasure in another's beauty. Paltry, nothing gestures, casual statements, flirting is healthy. So here was something new. And for whatever reason that was known only to her, she decided to examine the issue in New York, after we had been here for a full day, experienced some wonderful food, scenery, theater (well…), discussed eroticism in the arts, in public spheres, awoken to croissants which, amazingly enough, we rarely eat at home. Thank you, Ron. Perhaps tennis isn't my sport, I thought.

What were you doing with Bénédicte? she asked that next morning in the hotel. I didn't hesitate in my response, there was no time to reflect upon the nature of lies and the best way to go about telling them. I wanted to see her, I said. Why? I don't know, I just did, I had some time, I was off work early, there was nothing pressing at the office—this was true, it's usually the case, the flexibility of my working hours—I thought to pop by, say hello. Anna paused, as anyone in her predicament would. Why did you lie to Ron about the book? Now was a good time for reflection, this would require skill, care. I, too, paused. It was a mere reaction, I said. I felt awkward somehow, as though it would somehow be inappropriate for us to be together, alone, in her apartment. It seems absurd in retrospect, don't you think?

I don't believe you, Anna said.

There was something altogether crushing in the way she said this. In addition to the content of her statement aimed at my chest, perhaps my genitalia. Though the line between our eyes was equally direct, quite. What are you saying? I'm saying that I don't believe you, I feel that you are hiding something from me and I would like you to be honest. Anna, I said, your daughter is of no more concern to me than anyone else in my family—I stopped by to say hello, we covered over a potentially awkward situation with a book—I am much more anxious about you, your well-being, your happiness, our time in New York, of which we still have a day and half left. And only half of what I'm saying to you is a lie, I wanted to conclude, but, of course, I did not. Please don't think what you are thinking, I said. Anna was quiet during our walk in the city, we needed to walk, she needed to walk freely, without knowing where we were going, between a massive array of buildings that dwarfed her. There would be no metro ride today. Together and alone. She eventually took my hand. It's an impossible thought.

All of this followed by food, we passed a celebrity, piles of people in Times Square. And back into smaller burrows of New York, a quiet café, more walking. Our mutual lethargy seemed to ease the tension. We decided to return to the hotel early. We sat at the bar before it was overrun with people Bénédicte's age—except where the latter is concerned, I don't feel an enormous affinity for this demographic—we had drinks, alcohol further alleviated the strain between us. But Anna was not to be corralled—that awful livestock metaphor, I use it only because I'm not thinking clearly and because there is probably part of me that wants to do just that, to reign in her suspicions for the sake of my own selfish ends— she didn't look at me very much. She lived behind the austere polish of her lightness, her minimalism, back in our hotel room, the television turned on, our white noise maker on low. I found myself, incurably, stupidly at a time like this, envisioning the walls, the sheets, the light, the music, of Bénédicte's apartment. And the inhabitant whose presence adds genuine light there, rather than the weight of death, to the walls of my sinuous little being there, and anywhere, even in a hotel room with Anna. The presence of Bénédicte and the mutable frontiers of a dishonest man. It was hardly Anna's fault that her parents traumatized her by dying.

I read the collected works of the Czech poet once we returned from New York. Between meetings. At lunch. I admire his style, the unique way he writes his life and the ease with which he approaches difficult topics. I really know nothing of his political plight, only the small and large agonies of most people, and the pleasures of writing one's own existence in the everyday, the work that anyone does with more or less refinement, poetry, our various tools for constructing an original narrative of work, creation, food, sex, falling. I find the predictable, conventional narrative structure of a day in the life interminably dull.

Leave it to Lucille to ask the pertinent question. I found her in the middle of writing a business proposal. It's not her strong suit, business, but she's exceptionally good at what she does otherwise. Time in front of a computer, often home during the day. I was taking a lunch break. Bénédicte, sadly unavailable that afternoon. She was frustrated but welcomed me in, was thankful to see me, thank you for putting a temporary end to my torture, she said. She was wearing pajamas. I love Lucille. Perhaps I should be more careful about visiting women in their homes.

I don't have long, I said. But I need to talk to you. I told her about Bénédicte and Ron, Anna, New York, and the book of Czech poetry. She looked at me without speaking, without offering any impulse to speak, she just listened from her side of the sofa. Her home is much more colorful than Bénédicte's, or my own, for that matter. I told her that as disinterested as I am in hurting someone, or people—let's be honest, they're extensive, our tangled webs—things were beginning to break. Stories, trust, people. I just need to spit it out. I need advice, I said. She continued to look at me thoughtfully, still feeling the relief of not having to force a business proposal, I could tell, and finally she opened her mouth. She didn't speak immediately. She just opened her mouth, tossed her head back, moved her tongue around in her mouth, stroked her teeth. And then. Why don't you leave her? she stated. A rhetorical question. Naturally, I was a little embarrassed, even in front of Lucille, to ask who, which one? Anna, she said. I was thankful for that response. As though it somehow legitimized my affair, made it okay to be a reality. A reality that needs to be addressed, reconfigured, no doubt. But a reality that is, and, I cannot see any other way, will continue to be.

I said thank you with my eyes, though her own expression didn't change, her mouth still open slightly, her looking down on me from that angle, over her nice glasses, tongue. Of course, there was in fact the anticipation of an answer, I was expected to reply. I stopped thanking her with my eyes and contemplated why I have yet to leave Anna. My inclination was a thoughtfully delivered I don't know. My professors at university had been very good at offering this answer in a way that saved face by humanizing them. Which made them even more god-like. Lucille was interested in neither my humanity nor my deity. I thought, switched positions on the sofa. When I spoke she closed her mouth and met me at eye level, the Lucille I have known for so many years.

Because. I don't want her to experience any more death.

Lucille jumped on this without pause. What do you think she's experiencing as she wonders if her partner is having sexual relations with her daughter? Is that life? Yes, I said. It is. It's still life, it's painful and abominable but she's alive, living it out. If I leave, especially to be with Bénédicte, the loss may be too great. She may implode, die inside. You know what I mean. Lucille thought, was not unaware of my meaning. If she suspects you, she probably suspects me of knowing, she said. That's a horrible thought. You're horrible. She made a child's face as she said this, which let me know that I'm not actually horrible in her estimation. Just a lying fuck. Inhale, exhale.

My advice, she said after a moment of looking the other

way for a change. Talk to her, gently, compassionately. Let her know that you're unhappy. Let it unfold carefully but efficiently. Don't torment her with weakness. Don't underestimate her resilience, she's a strong woman. And if this all goes well, don't even contemplate moving in straight away with Bénédicte, don't even bring it up. That would be horrible. The face of an adult, Lucille. That would be cancer, she said.

There was really nothing more for me to say on the subject other than to thank her for her insights. I didn't leave right away. I got closer to Lucille on the sofa. Where we reminisced, fought off time together. I had to get back to work, she had a business proposal to complete. How's the baby? I asked.

Anna is attending a symposium in another city. She called after dinner, told me about the symposium, her experience of the city, people she met. We shared a pleasant conversation about our respective days, called one another funny names. With Anna, it's names rather than faces. Anna is not a little disappointed about being away at this time, the annual Nuit Blanche, when downtown explodes, in the middle of a cold winter, the thousands of people roaming the streets, entering art galleries, cinemas, experiencing performances, all through the night. It doesn't really get exciting until at least midnight. I myself, it must be confessed, am elated.

Later, Bénédicte and I meet on the corner of Sherbrooke and St. Laurent, grab hands, hug, it doesn't matter who might be watching, nobody's watching, everyone is immersed in the white night and its refined entertainments. This night has always made me think of a call to arms. The winter has its way with us, for so long, but tonight, tonight we'll celebrate, everyone, we'll unite our immense talents and do battle by inviting our enemy—it is an enemy, it can't be denied, it's February, a tsunami of cold—to celebrate with us, contribute to our festivities. Bénédicte is gorgeous, the shape of her face between the strands of hair sticking out from underneath her hat, her smile, everyone is happy tonight, her scarf, her elegant coat, boots, the enthusiasm that radiates from her, it's intoxicating to me and I know that I exude the same just from being with her, ensconced in the radiating aura of Bénédicte. We walk north on St. Laurent, slip a bit on the ice, hold tight. Someone older, my age, mistakes me for the politician, long since removed from public exposure. Leather pants are no longer an appropriate fashion statement. We enter a cinema where a friend of hers is giving a performance. How lovely to be inside, in the heat.

Inside, the line to the theater's entrance is vast, we simply merge with the conglomeration of people waiting. Bénédicte chats with some friends, introduces me by my name alone, no unnecessary designations here, her friends are nice, interesting to me, and the line begins moving. The one performing is playing music to accompany an abstract film about China. The music, too, is abstract, at once ethereal and grounding, I say to Bénédicte once the performance is underway. A kind of avant-garde worship service, I say to her. She doesn't find this comment particularly interesting. It goes on, unfolding at a measured pace, filling the room with sounds and images that light down upon us, a light, warm rain in the theater—she finds this description worthwhile—adding to the mystery of La Nuit Blanche. And it is a mystery, the night, our being together here, the joy that obscures obvious challenges. Tonight we care only about joy.

Outside, we stand in the cold with other people filing out of the theater. We remember our upcoming holiday, a tricky negotiation. It's been postponed. But solidified. Helsinki. I have business there, of all places. Tickets are less expensive than one would think now. The trip will happen in the early spring, when it's still cold but there are days when once notices the ice melting, the people crawling out of their shells. Bénédicte is fond of beaches. And I don't blame her. Mediterrenean warmth. But them's the breaks. She thought this was a completely ridiculous thing for me to say.

But here the night is getting darker, people have ingested substances, drinking, there is still ample light,

in the faces, emanating from street lamps, spaces in
which people meander, celebrate. It's very late. Bénédicte
coils her arm through mine as we walk the streets with
the others. In a side street boutique, off the main strip of
St. Laurent, we observe a performer in a mask changing
in and out of clothes, boutique clothes, the people
gathered around his actions in a circle. His penis comes
to dangle in front of an uncomfortable man. I would be
uncomfortable too, only because another's unfamiliar
sex—man, woman, animal—would be in such close
proximity to my face, making my distress part of the
performance. But I'm not that man. Bénédicte enjoys the
performance, it gives us plenty to talk about back on the
street, where I mention the play in New York. Bénédicte
doesn't want to hear about my time with Anna. It's
probably time to go. We're back in the car, my snow tires
are brand new, on our way to her apartment, dawn is fast
approaching. We'll say goodbye in the car rather than
later in the morning, after breakfast, a late night of our
bodies being entangled. Out of a curious, and yes, ironic,
respect for Anna while she's away. We'll say goodnight
here, abscond from what would surely be a session of
nice love-making in the night. There is something
domestically sacred about the night when Anna is away.
I watch Bénédicte as she climbs the perilously icy steps
to her door.

Anna and I had sex one last time. The kind of thing you don't know but intuit. Doubtless, Anna intuited this fact to a greater degree than I did, or could. Her penchant for sensing the present in its vast relation to the future. I'm not one to believe that women are necessarily more intuitive than men, that menstruating automatically affords them a sorcery of divination. I believe it's the kind of skill that can be cultivated. Anna has cultivated that skill.

There was a sadness in its slow movement, slow pleasure unfolding in the safety of our bedroom. Our familiar bodies, aging along the line of time, we have always been happily forgiving of the other's aging body, fat deposits, wrinkles, the less than supple quality of skin as it ages, moves toward death despite our efforts to keep fit, it's much more of a quiet celebration of one another, a gentle reassurance that we are, in fact, awake together. We occupied a minimum of positions, but more than one, in an effort to extract the pleasure that is always there in us, awaiting a touch to draw it out. What a wonderful way of seeing that. We, all of us, are harbingers of pleasure walking, working, seeing films, never far from being triggered in the presence of another, and perhaps alone, with special skill.

There was no music, it was late. Had there been music, I might have preferred the cliché of a Gymnopedie. Some clichés are persuasive. Saint-Saëns

would have been completely inappropriate. We listened
to one another's aging sex grunts, the sounds that don't
seem as though they would come from Anna when she's
dining at a table, staring out the window of an airplane
with unimpeded sunlight illuminating her features,
minutes before landing in New York, a New York taxi.
But she sounds them, without contrivance, without the
intent to make an impression of any kind, as elegantly
as I have come to expect, her body sounds are made all
the more beautiful by their spontaneity, her experience.
I'm comfortable. I know what to do and what to avoid,
in this moment in particular, our mutual familiarity, I
know everything except that this will be the last time we
cull the pleasure from one another's bodies, the shared
being that is Anna, myself, in this physical union. I only
sensed, vaguely, sadly, that this would be the last time
for that.

The sadness was fluid, it had the quality of blood
being drawn gradually into the needle. The needle was
there, the pressure of its insertion underneath our mutual
pleasure. And while evident underneath, a distinct
presence, it extracted something. It withdrew a sample
of our shared life, blood, that would not be regenerated,
we both felt it. And then further fluids, insertions.
Climax, a final, beleaguered thrust, hers as well as my
own, against the sadness, the great melancholic force not
to be outdone by a mere physical exchange, embodied

pleasure, our knowing one another. A mere attempt between Anna and myself, after the lights had gone out, the books had been placed on the bedside table, to live together.

My philosophy is very simple. Just as one might think of pleasure being inherent, always already awaiting the nudge of someone's touch, or one's own private expression of the many layers of pleasure available to a life—the real truthfulness of one's being, a gleeful ontology—just as pleasure is innate to that being, so too is a certain alertness to life forever at hand. An improvised responsiveness that when adhered to in all of its spontaneity reveals an order. This is how it was once put to me, more or less, by another. She said, stand back, observe, act when necessary. Be at ease. Ease, I said. Yes, don't be an imbecile. It's easy to be imbecilic. Hard to observe. It's profoundly difficult to stand at a distance from it all. All? All, she said. I don't know exactly what she meant by observe, imbecility—I have many preoccupations in life that require thought in different directions, many pulling constraints, I don't always have time to figure things out—but I've made it my philosophy nonetheless. And I've found that it works. It leans me more towards contentment than despair. Perhaps it has something to do with laughter. A constant undercurrent of spontaneous, rooted laughter.

But when Anna speaks to me with the force of her anxiety, as she does on rare occasions, about some problem between us, some egregious trespass on one of our parts, and speech eventually becomes silence, when we argue, I am forced into a state of compliance with the civilized but no less dire condition of a lover's surveillance. The unspoken words between us, already spoken, informing the stillness that holds us captive in that stalemate of being together, being watched by one another, our shared conflict in that moment, silent arguing. For there is nowhere to turn in such moments, to go, even in thought, without the knowledge that the other is peering into me as I look away, my attempt to escape this moment between us, into the reaches of a landscape on the other side of the window, at the infinitesimal details of an object opposite my partner. She is looking into me, seeking an answer, or some acknowledgement that she is safe, staring. I can only think of power in these moments. The way it sits beside me, vanquished, and watches. Works its way into me with its eyes, faint, drained, but somehow resilient in its effort to apprehend the truth of a matter. From all sides. The power to bounce back if only I will comply with its needs to stare back and receive its features, facial gestures intended to provoke sympathy. She stares at me, in the face of some matter dividing us, for extended periods in hopes of eliciting the truth. A stare to which

I often succumb, partly because I love Anna, I desire her highest good. And partly because being watched in such a manner is a nuisance. A condition to move through with care, agility, great velocity. An element of this in our final night of love-making.

That's quite a view, I said to the boy sitting next to me on the plane. The plane was approaching Helsinki. Below us we could see the sea meeting land, and closing further in on the city, the massive Lutheran cathedral, the island of Suomenlinna fortress, another cathedral. The boy was less interested in looking than I was in showing. I continued, unimpeded by his indifference, to point things out. It had been a long journey. The boy and I had been neighbors since New York, since my layover in New York. I hoped that his situation would eventually mirror my own as a youth, the acne having cleared itself up by the time women became an inestimable priority. Bénédicte would take a later flight, two days later, mostly to avoid suspicion, enough time for me to attend to business matters, visit friends, encounter the city on my own again. She would even call her mother on the day of her departure, to say hi, no, not much happening, and then catch a taxi to the international airport.

Helsinki, the Pearl of the Baltic. Yes. Though what one discovers is that any number of places, different countries, lay claim to this title. Lots of pearls strung along

the Baltic Sea. Unique climate, landmasses, populated
by people who have adapted to their surroundings over
many years and thus cultivated their uniqueness in the
world. It's a climate that is not unfamiliar to me. But
there is no reason to deny Helsinki its right to be a pearl.
As is the case with other cities, there is a wonderful
juxtaposition here between the older and the newer,
grand old architectures (Helsingin rautatieasema, the
main train station) jutting up against slickly modern
design (Kiasma, the Museum of Contemporary Art). The
polished genius of Alvar Aalto. And the architecture of
people, their reservation, and their suspicion informing
a first, possibly a second meeting, the manner in which
they suspect the other of being too uncomfortably other.
The stereotype is true, as it happens, that the average
Finn is not a quick friend. But once one secures that
friendship, barring the common tragedies of neurosis,
natural disaster, one has that friend for life. This has
been my experience. I pondered my friendships here
after waving goodbye to the boy who seemed to have
embarked on a specialized course of study. I suppose,
in retrospect, that the time of sexual obsession had long
since begun for him. Perhaps he is here to escape it, I
thought.

   I enjoy being alone. In the city, enveloped by that
air of bristling elation that only city life can produce—
the countryside has its own euphoria, I don't want to be

misunderstood here—roaming the streets once one has settled into the particular rhythm, remembering street names, not so difficult to pronounce once one grasps the relatively consistent pronunciation. A surprising number of people out, given the cold, rich colors, though mainly darks, black coats, winter wear, Bénédicte will be pleased, she'll likely want to buy me something and I won't refuse unless it's just too tight. The tendency to reflect, in solitude, upon one's self as a person of color, light or dark shades, gender, one's history and one's future, relations, one's primary project in life, the now of reflection that is made all the more liminal by the condition of being alone in a city.

Negotiating the weather. Not unlike what I'm accustomed to, certainly, but still. One is away, on holiday, one wishes to be as free as possible to move, enjoy the scenery without too much interference. This level of cold can be constricting. At once forcing the vacationer to move, keep the body flowing, and freezing his limbs, her face, nose hairs. Such that movement is very much a compromised affair. My thermals probably need to be replaced, I thought, but Bénédicte will only want to buy me something nice for the exterior. Which I understand. We can each take care of the long underwear on our own. I walked along the streetcar line and contemplated what I might pick out for Bénédicte, a kind of welcome to our holiday gift upon her arrival.

The anticipation of which I was able to balance nicely with solitary meanderings in the heart, and eventually, on the outskirts of the great wintry pearl.

It gets ugly beyond the city center. Like many cities. There's more dirty snow, less attention paid to manicuring the sidewalks. It's only somewhat different in summer. Beyond Espoo, and a little before. I don't know what I'm doing out here, I thought. Looking for something new. An adventure. And the business meeting, a fair ways outside the core of the precious Baltic gem. We had dinner, Finnish colleagues, they've become my lifelong friends over the years, such a pleasure to see them, back in the center of the city, a fine restaurant, we drank together. Mika, the boss, my longest associate and friend here, made a splendid toast, to me, his friend, who brings such joy to business, to Finland. It was characteristically sentimental. And as with the climate, I am not unfamiliar with this manner of operation.

I am not predisposed to Finnish cuisine, there is little in my own culture that would make me naturally inclined to enjoy the Finnish menu without effort on my part. There's fish, of course. Nail the salmon cut to a small board, place it at the edge of a fire, in the wilderness, a succulent forest dish. And guidebooks will mention berries (cloudberries, they make excellent jam, on ice cream, when the mood strikes, sure, why not), Karelian pies (compelling once, twice), reindeer (culturally difficult to stomach, one thinks of eating Koala bear, kitten, playful monkey, but tasty), but the day to day reality, outside the lavish restaurant, the dinner party, is split pea soup and potatoes. Blood sausage, sickening. Even as Mika articulated such a poetic toast, I remembered missing cream, freshness, a rare croissant, Cuisine du Terroir with a little high flair added for good measure, in the night, from before. I suppose we have our foie gras, no less repugnant to this palette, let me be very clear. Mika is one of the loveliest men I have ever encountered.

As Bénédicte entered the common area for international arrivals, I was struck by the ease with which she moved through the crowd. Her bag wheeling behind her, her traveling clothes simple, elegant. She knows how to move, to walk, many people don't, her early training as a dancer. There's nothing more perfect than Bénédicte, I thought. Except perhaps the degree to which some exceptional individuals circumvent imbecility. I'd thought about making a silly sign for her but the time of being alone in Helsinki had made me a bit too reflective for that. The presence of Bénédicte would surely change this for me. We enjoy being silly together, even though the mood that most commonly pervades our time in one another's company is closer to calm reverence. We revere one another. That's why I'm with her. We listen to one another. We respond. The play of our critical exchanges. I trust that what she says, how she sits, emotes, is the truth of her in that moment, and perhaps the truth of something larger, barring the fleeting persona of an actress. There are few phenomena in life more nauseating than two people in closeness, living intimately, who don't believe in the truth of one another, at any given moment. After we embrace, we don't say anything, she looks at me squarely—we're nearly the same height—and she smiles her own smile, it belongs to no one else, a knowing expression. We know nothing of time. She's happy to be with me in Helsinki. No censure whatsoever. And she says, hi ya pops.

In the hotel room there's a lot of kissing, fondling, an explosion of uninterrupted affection. No one is going to call (well, Anna) or stop by, no fathers—mine is dead—we relish these times of complete freedom together. To lock hands, limbs. I've reached the point in my life where I'm generally more interested in the slow emulsion of two bodies and their heightened sensitivity than I am in the rush to penetration, or the rush to hard fast thrusting. Age has made me sensitive in this way. Bénédicte will on occasion force the rush, and this is fine, perfectly fine. I remain capable of all modes of performance, durability, passion. It's amazing that the city of Helsinki, or anything else for that matter, exists outside our hotel room as we vanish into and resurface from one another.

The phone rang. We looked at one another without joy. We must answer, there's no telling who, what it could be, we'll spend the rest of the day wondering. It was the concierge. We would like to offer you a complimentary bottle of Port. We know how you like it, we've come to know your taste, monsieur. Please give me an hour before delivering it to the room, and thank you, thanks so much, this is very thoughtful, I said. I gave Bénédicte her gift before the Port arrived. To be witnessed only by Bénédicte and myself.

We went to dinner. Bénédicte has never been to Finland. I ordered for the both us this time, as in the game with Lucille. It was a nice restaurant, I've been here many times. No bloody sausage, no dreary potatoes. We each had a glass of wine with dinner, only one, remembering that the Port awaited us back at the hotel, a late night dessert, chocolate. There was nothing pushing us to get up early beyond the pleasure of occupying the city. Bénédicte wanted to visit the Kiasma and the indoor market, Kauppatori, by the harbor. And oh, there's a film festival this weekend. Only after dinner, once the Port began to settle, did the jetlag catch up with Bénédicte. We would sleep well, make love again in the morning.

Hotel dining/lounge areas are unique spaces, always the same ambience, foreign yet uniquely familiar. We sat there, waking up, enjoying the unnatural light that battles the dark morning outside, an English newspaper shared between us, tea, pastries. This may not be the healthiest long weekend of eating. And in general we soaked up that sense of Scandinavian otherness there, along with a few others, Finns, and others of different nationalities, a quiet first morning together in Helsinki.

The misfortune first appeared to Bénédicte, her knack for noticing such things—and really, the same could be said of most anyone being followed—after we had lingered a little longer than we had planned in the dining/lounge area with our paper and our nourishment. The Port, the chocolate from the night before having taken the very toll we expected them to take. She noticed him staring, not completely unheard of in a hotel environment, even one of this caliber. The heightened interest people take in people while traveling, celebrity searching, even in Finland. And something about her sense of things there told her that the staring was on the verge of crossing boundaries that are more or less universal. She whispered for me to— look—without being obvious, which I did. An average enough guy, nothing exceptional about his appearance, his demeanor, staring. And then I began to feel what Bénédicte was feeling. Discomfort. He probably should have stopped looking our way several minutes ago. We left the hotel for the day's outing. Bundled up.

The film festival didn't start until the next day, so we would make do with modern art, some shopping,

Kauppatori, a touristic café, a lighter dinner, and we'll see about the Port again, in the night, before bed. We spoke about modern art throughout our tour of each room in the Kiasma, Bénédicte is quite insightful on this large topic. I know what many people know about modern art, perhaps a little more, but no more than that. She made me feel something in front of certain pieces. It wasn't just her explanation, her body, there, the speaking mouth that has been so gentle and so cunning with my member for a number of years now, all over my body, really, it was the way she illuminated the art, brought its power—yes, its aura—into a perspective that I would not have recognized otherwise. She made the art speak. And I listened because much of the art I found compelling and because it was speaking, in part, through the mouth of the woman for whom I would do almost anything. I'm fortunate in that she is very good at telling me what she wants. A rich, cool, blue light glistening in spaces of the museum, and elsewhere, clear white walls, not unlike Bénédicte's apartment, even the architecture of the museum is elevated, a universe away from pedestrian ideas, banal concerns. We stayed there longer than we had planned, there would be a limited amount of time for shopping today. I asked Bénédicte if she would prefer to have lunch at Café Kiasma or to walk a bit and join the other tourists at the Strindberg Café.

It is not entirely out of the question that one might overhear a discussion of the café's namesake, assuming that one can understand the language, in the packed, beautiful interior, or on the sidewalk, among the many tables on the street Pohjoisesplanadi, in the summer, at the Strindberg Café. Just as one might hear talk of an older gentleman and a fish, or boxing, in a Café Hemingway. A fatwa, in Café Rushdie, while having tea, coffee, a pastry. Bénédicte and I spoke about Strindberg's *Miss Julie*, which Anna and I saw onstage some years back. I attempted to explain how mesmeric this production was, the impact of its power play between the young but aristocratic Miss Julie and Jean, the valet. The insinuation that Miss Julie's only way out of socially inappropriate desire and the emptiness of being an 18th century woman in Sweden was to kill herself, with a razor, sure, and the sense that this was precisely what she was off to do in the final act, curtain. But Bénédicte remained skeptical of theater. Obviously the play had nothing to do with us, our desire, social strictures. To further celebrate our holiday, we decided on special coffee drinks, whipped cream, completely against our routine. Bénédicte made a funny gesture with her hand. I made a face at her.

Bénédicte made another gesture with her hand. I realized she was gesturing towards something, someone. She thought, of course, that she had spotted the strange man from the hotel, peering at her through the window. I saw no one like that. I even began to question whether the man from earlier had really acted so inappropriately. She had clearly been pondering his significance throughout the day. I attempted to ease her mind. I told her that I love her. I am so profoundly in love with you, my Bénédicte. I get over it, but it's a little painful sometimes, how much I adore you between the barbed wires of our daily lives. She placed her hand on mine, with nothing to separate us there, in the café, and said that she feels the same.

Dinner, in the late evening, after having walked the cold streets, crunched snow under our boots. And then he really did turn up. That was him, alone. At the restaurant, seated a few tables away. That he was staring was beyond question. It was even difficult to eat. Bénédicte was particularly frustrated. Bénédicte, I said, he probably thinks you're the actress, whose name I still couldn't recall. Of course he does, she said. Her frustration was not far from manifesting as an attack on me. I didn't blame her. It must be hard to be famous, a celebrity in a city where people may already be predisposed to seek you out, your kind, the entertainers of the planet. Mythical creatures. Though not a little beguiled by the resemblance, tonight Bénédicte just wanted to enjoy her meal. At one point I endeavored to confront the intrusion of his staring with my own, looking him square in the eye. But I couldn't hold it as long as he did. I lost the match. Another worthy opponent. We left without dessert, I did everything I could to talk up some more fine Port, perhaps something fun on television, a film back at the hotel—the film festival begins tomorrow! I said, as though I had forgotten and remembered—how nice it is to lie in bed and watch a film together, I said. But he knows we're staying at the hotel, she said. Yes, it's true, but we can be private and happy in our room. Prisoners, she said.

At which point she, my Bénédicte, my beloved, flashed a look that signified loss. That's the best way to describe this look. Or lack, supreme lack. To the extent that I could read her thought, I know this look, have held it on a number of occasions. As though I was completely and profoundly other. I know you, my blood, my closest friend, and yet you are, in this instant, a foreign entity. We are all alone. What's one to do? Scream. Or sit quietly, wait for it to pass.

I must admit to having become a little frustrated here. There's as much to suspect as there is to honor in such moments. Especially the case when one feels imprisoned, stalked. She saw my own frustration, and in perfect Bénédicte fashion, looked straight at the man with precisely the expression of the actress, held it, the intensity of her censure, with nothing to stop her, her fury. And very quickly, I could hardly believe it, he abruptly turned away, left. She had annihilated him, there in the restaurant. A realist, I suggested that he might be waiting for us outside. Probably, she said. Fuck him.

He did wait for us. Then followed us back to the hotel. I was right. Another delightful evening in our spacious room, something nice to drink, intimacy, a film screening in advance of tomorrow's festival. I made a mental note to purchase some Port back home, for sleep, and to retain the memory of being here on this cold night, secluded with my beloved.

I'd never been to the cinema in Helsinki. A brief walk towards Eerikinkatu took us to the Orion, the city's repertoire theater, a wonderful, wonderful space, a kind of museum to the living, thriving art of cinema, not so far from our hotel. The lobby was packed, Finns, mostly, though there are always many foreigners in Helsinki, other Europeans, some Americans, students, people from all over. Bénédicte and I enjoyed browsing through the film schedule and choosing what stood out to us. We enjoyed looking at all the people dedicated to film, also eager to be met by a deluge of moving images, in the darkened space, a community of film lovers. People occasionally glanced at Bénédicte as though she might be someone they recognized. It ended up being less a conventional festival and more a conglomeration of films, some new to the Orion's collection, being screened in a marathon few days. As usual, she depended on me to purchase our tickets, to speak Finnish, which I do with certain pronounced limitations.

Our first film was Danish, very beautiful, sublime acting, dense drama. We both felt at once a little shitty and uplifted by the film once it concluded and we exited the theater to remember that we're not those people, our lives are moving forward in relative smoothness, calm. Of course, we could become those people. So many choices. We discussed the film at length, the cinematography, the consequences of certain directorial choices, at a café down the street, lunch. The next one was early evening, a must, a Hitchcock neither of us had seen. How perfect, I said. Yes, she said. Rather than try three in one day, we took the afternoon off, walked west toward water, a cemetery, always provocative of reflection, a fitting scene following the Danish film. We walked on water just beyond the cemetery, ice.

Hitchcock was so extraordinary at finding that space between enthralling entertainment and the artfulness of film. It's been said before. But it isn't until one enters a film, its sacred space, that this fact really speaks to you. It spoke to us, there, at the Orion, as it did to many others, applause at the end, for a dead man, a long absent director. Those moments of anxiety, identifying with characters in and out of trouble, terrible trouble in some cases, what Bénédicte called scopophilia, the mode of identification thought by some to dictate the psychology of the average film viewer. We enjoyed every moment of the Hitchcock, were elated upon leaving the darkened room, smiled at people, our mutual celebration of a fat genius.

We both found the irony, then, of the strange man staring at Bénédicte in the lobby, immediately following the thriller, to be not a little wondrous, funny. But soon the reality of being stalked set in, his was not a particularly pleasant face. And though Bénédicte clearly had the power to stare him down, he seemed to be growing stronger, braver, in this regard. He edged closer to us, closer than ever, and continued staring, transfixed by Bénédicte. He seemed to absorb her power. It occurred to me that it was time to act rather than to flee. I whispered in her ear, explained my plan, what would amount to a whopping serve, an ace, I was confident, using the energy of my aggravation. A man must act, he must do something. I walked over to him.

You really need to stop following us, I said—forever the equanimous Borg, I had even allowed my beard to grow out somewhat—it's inconsiderate. Please leave us be or I shall be forced to. To which he responded, he interrupted, without consideration for my equanimity. You will never be me, he said.

I stared back at him for the briefest of moments, overtly flustered, he had decimated me. Instead of pulling my carcass off the ground, taking a final stand, with a fist, or more likely, wit—I didn't want to cause a scene in the Orion—I stepped back to Bénédicte. We need to call the police, I said. Her unhappiness was not small.

The pleasure of our evening together, over a late dinner, back at the hotel, where he was probably camped out, was understated.

The next morning, I alerted the police to our predicament. The policewoman suggested we drop by the station. Well, we're on holiday, I said. Yes but you never know, she said. I spent a significant portion of the morning convincing Bénédicte that the police station was a good idea because you never know. That it wouldn't take long, and it didn't. There we were met with the utmost respect and consideration. We were directed to the office of Detective Kokkonen. Call me Kari, he said. He looked at us, and especially at Bénédicte, with great interest. Another lovely, if somewhat guarded, Finnish man. He was, after all, a detective. Bénédicte commented on the alliteration of his name in a private whisper. Your story, he said, is cause for some concern. It's probably nothing, he assured us, but one can't be too careful. Familiar detective words, it seemed to me. Kari asked us if we wouldn't mind being followed by a detective. He himself would do the following, just for a few hours. We're already being followed by one person, Bénédicte said, her annoyance readily apparent, why not one more. Kari looked at us both and smiled. Tell me where you're going and when, he said paternally. He was roughly my age.

We walked along an esplanade by a park, over to Bulevardi and up Fredrikinkatu before ending up back at the cinema. What would prove to be our third and last film of the weekend event. A French film, as it happened, how nice not to have to pay attention to subtitles. Common themes, shared sensibilities. A wonderful film, it turned out to be, but not before Kari, with the help of our subtle gestures, located the strange man, he was there, of course, watching the French film, or not. Fantasizing about Bénédicte in the dark. Thus beginning the end of our holiday's intrigue.

When the film was over—we spoke passionately about the film despite unforeseeable events, a stalker, the potentially violent intervention of the authorities, Charlotte Rampling is capable of sublime performance— we took a cue from Kari and proceeded out the door, down Runeberginkatu all the way to Sibeliuksenpuisto. A very long walk to see the Sibelius monument. Kari wanted to tire the strange man. Neither Bénédicte nor I are especially interested in the music of Sibelius, though who would disagree that *Finlandia* is a moving anthem? Kari's instinct was correct. The strange man grew not only weary, along with his prey, but rancorous, a little volatile. He began yelling at Bénédicte. And at me. Mostly at me. You can never be me, he yelled, you are a nothing, a piece of shit, she only has eyes for me, she has proved it over and over again. This was enough for Kari to accost the man after calling for back up. Back up arrived as we admired the monument. They pinned him down, handcuffs, more yelling from this man with whom we shared one final endearing glance before he told Bénédicte that he loved her. She's not who you think she is, I said. He looked at me, baffled.

It turned out that the man had a record, and a warrant for his arrest. He was wanted. The sight of Bénédicte had pushed him to out himself, a number of terrible crimes. Bénédicte and I held one another. We couldn't believe it, that this was our holiday. I doubt that she has ever felt the same about her resemblance to the actress. Once the man was taken away, Kari remained with us, standing in the cold by the Sibelius monument, it was quite moving, witnessing the degradation of that man, his life in our midst. Kari recognized the relatively shattered quality of our holiday and, in another unexpected turn of events, invited us to dine in his home. Piia, his wife, would love to meet us. He beamed at Bénédicte when he said this, like a father. We would be honored to have you as our guests. Impossible to refuse.

The first time I visited Helsinki, an atrocious crime occurred. Two police officers were executed by a lone gunman, a Russian, as it turned out. I remember it well. The news was abuzz with details, grief, people grieving throughout the country, people placing flowers at the site of the shooting. That I, along with the rest of the country, remember this so clearly is a testament to the otherwise relative safety of Helsinki. Due in no small part, I imagine, to the work of crime fighters such as Kari, and to the restrictions on gore and violence allowed on Finnish television programming. They do allow, it must be noted, nudity to appear on prime time.

Kari dropped us off at our hotel to change from our walking clothes to something a bit more formal, for dining, take your time, he said, I'll call ahead to Piia, have a coffee in the lounge. What does one wear to the home of a detective? asked Bénédicte in the room. I suggested we dress down and save our best clothes for the following night, our last in Helsinki. Our last night. The thought struck me as a bit disappointing and I felt the need to ask her why she loves me. She turned, slowly, without surprise, and contemplated the question. There is no one like her. I understand that the plethora of interesting people on the planet dwarfs the marvel of Bénédicte, but for me, there is really, and finally, no one else to move me the way she does, make me feel at ease, aware of the grandeur of my nothing life. He was right, the stalker, I'm a nothing. I became afraid that she would again pierce me with that look of isolation, my fear that she would begin to succumb to such moments, unlike most of us who forget, move on. Because you are both father and lover, she said finally. She said this. And before I could take offense, she laughed and said, I love you because you care, listen, inquire. She draped one leg over my knees, on the bed. You have the quality—she emphasized the word—of a father, my own, in fact, and your love, your love-making, is real.

I accepted this, I let it play in my thoughts as we continued getting ready, headed to the lounge where Kari was talking with a member of the hotel staff. I wanted to abandon the dinner and stay in with Bénédicte, rip her out of her nice but not her best clothes, be inside of her, quickly, and then slowly, but there was no way out now. A day of various textures, oscillating frequencies.

It wasn't until we had been there for a while, in the gracious home of Kari and Piia, who could not have been more delightful, in that beautifully mannered, Finnish way, that I realized Kari probably harbored a silent conviction that Bénédicte was in fact the actress, operating under a different name. Piia, too, seemed especially taken by the presence of Bénédicte. Whether my beloved was aware of this during the dinner, I don't know, we didn't discuss it, we were both tired of the actress and the ongoing misrecognition. The couple was innocent enough though, Kari's paternal detective quality continued to take shape, suggestions of things to do in Helsinki, his sharing of stories, photographs of his life with Piia. There emerged the typical dynamic of two heterosexual couples, Kari brought me into his office to show off a collection of old rock and roll albums—would you like to listen? Oh, no thank you, I said, grinning—while Bénédicte and Piia talked in the living room.

And later, the four of us reconvened, would you like to go to sauna? Bénédicte and I looked at one another without a single answer between us, nothing, just confusion—sauna is the one Finnish tradition in which I've miraculously not taken part during my travels here—so Kari answered for us. He left the room to get some towels, told us where we could change, in the shower room, and beside that, a door just off the sauna, where you can slip outside, there's a bench, feel the cold after the warmth. He told us how to work the sauna once the stones are properly heated. Piia got us each a beer and spoke of the sacred quality of the sauna. And then it all happened so fast, Bénédicte and I holding towels, removing our clothes, wondering, somewhere in the backs of our minds, if this wasn't some kind of swinging arrangement, but knowing that it was merely time to sit in extreme heat, alone, be with one another.

The first scoop of water I threw on the rocks was too much. Naked in someone else's home, we both clenched our faces, they seemed to be melting off, and Bénédicte suggested that she handle the water from that point on.

But once the steam dissipated, there was that tranquility to which Piia alluded, sweat pouring from our bodies, the immense quietude of the small room, the two of us alone together in a way that we had never been, it felt to me. I stroked her face, her neck, her breasts, we vowed to do this again sometime, make love in the sauna, we sipped our beer. Bénédicte threw more water on the stones. The steam rising, there's nothing like this. Not that we made love at this juncture, in this sauna. Bénédicte stroked my back. We melted into the heat, stayed that way, a sense of worship in the enclosed sanctuary of heat, and coming to know that purity of body that the Finns have cultivated over many years of occupying such sacred space.

And then, of course, the heat becomes a bit much, it was time to exit. We asked each other without speaking if we should step outside. It seemed nuts. Minus fifteen out there. But why not. With towels around our bodies, mine a bit lower on the body, we stepped into the cold, sat on the bench on which Piia had placed a clean towel. A ways outside the city center, enough to get a sense of the sky, stars. It was freezing. But after sauna, one is able to withstand the cold, it comes as an invigorating blast of life following the heat. We enjoyed the beer. We sat close to one another, my arm around her, and before the shivering began, before showering off, getting back into our clothes, before Kari offered to give us a lift to the hotel and I insisted on calling a taxi, our time in bed after a long, unexpected day in Helsinki, under the open sky brightened by the lights of the city, I told Bénédicte that I was happy. Me too, she said. Bénédicte had never seemed more genuine to me. More capable of channeling authenticity, love. She flexed a leg muscle. I told her, again, how happy I am.

Our last day. Light, unnatural light in the northern darkness making shops and galleries, cafés, brighter, more naturally daytime than they would otherwise appear. Apparently, the suicide rate in Finland, contrary to what one might suppose, rises in the summer, when the sun blares for so long and only becomes the haziest approximation of night for a few hours. Too much luminosity for some. Or too much summer ease, easy pleasure. I really don't understand it, suicide. So we soaked up whatever light we could, enjoyed the novelty of the darkness, the cold that really isn't so different from the cold we know at home, tea.

And in the night, after dinner, a bar that Bénédicte had heard about, Erottaja. It was full of students, art students, I suspect, and a few older drinkers. Great music, colors, dark ambience that felt somehow, exceptionally European, it was underground, near the city center, but it could have been a secret gathering spot for marginalized artists in Berlin, years ago. I loved the name. The other side of pure bodies in sauna. Minimal beats, people in clothes, fashion, Europe being at once old and provocatively young. I said that she had made a good choice for our final night. Bénédicte appreciated the fact that I am only getting old on my skin.

In the night, in bed, I sometimes wish to fall asleep as quickly as possible so as to begin a new day, to accelerate the pace of moving toward her once again, an opportunity to speak to, if not see Bénédicte during an afternoon break, lunch. On our last night, I fell asleep peacefully, she was coiled around me, at least until we needed to separate, it was a large, comfortable bed, there were no strange men lurking after us. In the morning we would fly back home and begin more of our life together in the shadows. But light, everywhere. Light as our guide through this journey of what I, during these trips together, away from our tangled webs in another north, nearly forget to call deception.

The flight was long. Not so bad, but it's typically quite long on the way back, after the holiday has been lived, people met, oddities of people, occurrences, architecture. Once the layover in Amsterdam was complete, we settled into the flight, an unwatchable film on the screen, headphones that don't always stay in one's ears, and views. We slept a bit, or Bénédicte slept. I have difficulty sleeping on flights but am generally interested enough in what's happening around me to keep from being bored. Or I read. In retrospect, I was serious about bringing more fiction into my life. The intrusion of Ron had precipitated the intention, I need more of that in my life, particularly on the evenings when I'm away from his daughter, when there is very little chance of our speaking until the following day. I had purchased a book in Helsinki, at a used bookshop, plenty of English, some French. I read while Bénédicte slept. Eventually, I also drifted to sleep, though it had nothing to do with the book. I was tired and gratified.

Bénédicte held me close again when the pilot announced our arrival, please stay seated, wait, thanks for flying. She walked ahead of me down the aisle of the jet, trying not to smash into people with her bag, and reattached herself to me in the corridor that leads to the gate, that very peculiar atmosphere prior to entering the airport proper, that Orwellian corridor. We held hands, on our way to the baggage claim. We waited with the others from our flight, looked at them one last time before dispersing forever, the traveling companions with whom we could very well have perished, as sometimes happens with flights, the quiet intensity of that relationship, more present for some than for others in mid-flight. I rarely think about it. The bags arrived in spite of our wondering if they would in fact arrive, or if we would have to speak to someone at a special desk, point to generic bags that resemble ours, give our addresses, more waiting for the airline to correct its mistakes, wait to use our toothbrushes, wear our clothes. We walked hand in hand to find a taxi, the exit bustled with people moving in different directions, or standing still, standing confused, in the way.

We spotted Anna before she spotted us. And then the moment of her seeing us, very much what she expected, it seemed. Anna was there waiting for us. She saw us and stopped. She stood and stared, another person in the way of other people trying to get to where they were going. Except that Anna was grounded. A boulder that exists in one place and one place alone because nature has put it there in all of its immensity. People walked carefully around her. Her devastation like the force of gravity. Quite far from our own being there, in that moment, still holding our bags but no longer holding hands. Ours was a relatively scattered position among the people who bumped us in their efforts to get by. Bénédicte began to shake, I tried to hold her, to comfort her, but she resisted, kept staring at her mother without any of the power she had manifested to stare at the stalker, and lost. I didn't know where to aim my vision. I felt murdered. Until Bénédicte ran off, into the crowd. I reached out for her, missed. It was all happening with blitzing speed, and then with inconceivable lingering. Anna, myself and our bags still motionless. I watched Bénédicte until she was out of sight, as though that would somehow bring her back, let's sit, talk this through for a moment, the three of us, for Christ's sake, I thought. But she was gone. And when I turned back, Anna had also disappeared, without my noticing, by the time I turned to her, in search of I don't know what.

I stood, finally, and for once, myself, a listless, weighted stone.

Mais maintenant, dans ce moment, en cela très maintenant, la graine du plaisir interminable.

THREE

L ucille has miscarried. It happened while we were away. Anna told me while we were together, briefly, at home. I've gone to Lucille, not knowing what to expect. She's so light, she has experienced the profound loss of a parent, disappearing men, a wilted relationship, but this seems different. Anna said it's been difficult. It hurts me to know that I wasn't there for her when it happened. She'll forgive me, there's nothing to forgive, she'll say, I know her, but still. I wonder if she told Anna that I was not alone on my trip.

I went to see her. When she answered the door, I could see her strength, a transparent sheen over otherwise lifeless features, I moved in to embrace her, held her there, longer than when we shared a bed, our bodies, many years ago. I held her until she let go, pulled away, closed the door behind us. She asked mechanically if I would like anything. Let's sit, I said. We sat next to one another, her comfortable sofa. I noticed tissues on the coffee table. You don't have to talk, you don't have to do or say anything. I'm here with you as long as you want me to stay, I said. A non-committal smile from Lucille. She asked again if I would care for something, tea, water, juice. How about juice, I said. She said there is orange and cranberry. How about a mixture of both, I say. I could hear her in the kitchen, fumbling through a cabinet, pouring, I half expected her to come back in tears but she reappeared, a stronger smile now, her hand was steady as she set the glass on a coaster. I'm happy to see you, she said. What happened? I asked.

She didn't speak immediately. But I sensed that she wanted to speak, eventually, when it felt right, when she felt safe in doing so. She sat thinking, retreated into her thoughts. We sat in silence together while I drank my juice.

I don't believe, she said finally, that I deserved that. I said of course you didn't, and then felt awkward for interrupting what was more speculative, more philosophical than pity-seeking. She didn't respond to me directly.

I knew there was something wrong—I had decided to keep it, you know—that morning. I felt it in my body.

And then there was too much blood, it's natural, some blood, but not like that. It was clumpy, it had too much texture, I didn't know what to do. I called Anna. She was home, she insisted we go to the clinic but the clinic wasn't open, there was only the hospital. She was calm, she was wonderful. She picked me up and when we arrived there was a wait, surprise, and finally I was given a room, a makeshift room. A doctor listened to me speak about the morning, and then to my belly, and he expressed concern. He said I would have to wait a while. I nearly fell asleep, with Anna beside me in a chair. At one point, she stepped out to use the bathroom but I suspected she was having words with the doctor. I did fall asleep, I was tired from whatever medication they had given me and from worrying about what was going to happen. I was then to be moved to another room, though not before a transitional period, in the hall, on a gurney, among others, also waiting to be seen. I felt like I had gotten to know the others in the hall without speaking to them, those shared moments of intensity, uncertainty, agony, for some. Anna remained. Then came the moment when I asked Anna to walk me to the bathroom. I was weak. She stood outside. There were two teenagers there, just outside the bathroom, a young couple. I don't know why they were there. It was the male, I think, who seemed to be the patient. There was no nurse or doctor to help, in the hall, the bathroom. Anna stood outside until I cried out for her.

Lucille continued speaking and I soon understood that she was right. She shouldn't have gone through this. There was a density of experience here, there is a mass of unnecessary suffering in this experience for her, she's entirely too good for this, I thought.

I cried a bit as she elaborated on what had happened, the moment of miscarriage. I had never done that with her—Lucille had been unable to attend my sibling's funeral—she, too, began to cry. It isn't right to be assaulted with that kind of anguish, that contemptuous lack of a tender gesture, the calm presence of Anna notwithstanding, I thought. It's okay, she had said to herself in the hospital bathroom, this is going to be fine, know this about yourself, your child. Strength, optimistic thoughts. Though she couldn't finally adapt herself to such thoughts in the moment of real crisis, there was nothing there for her other than the experience of ruin, an unforgiving moment.

So it broke out of her. On a toilet. Part of her that had been growing. That which had compelled her to study, read books, share stories with others who would likely not be broken in a hospital bathroom. Lucille's child. The father had no idea. The teenagers just outside, and the others milling about, curious about the noises coming from the bathroom, the shattered moaning mother, Anna speaking softly, knew more than he did.

And then, a tranquility of sorts. She explained to me. More medication, on a table, in another wing, a quiet space, away from others in dire emergency. Monitoring Lucille's condition after the fact. The nurses were kind and gentle, Anna still with her, for as long as she needed. There was counseling available, more meds, home.

I apologized to Lucille for crying. She laughed at me, she took my hand and looked away, there was really nothing more to say about what happened. We enjoyed the silence together, after she had spoken, the voicing of this event between us was now accomplished. A sense of relaxation after our going through that together, to the best of our ability following the lived event. It will continue to be lived, she knew. She is resilient, Lucille. We are much alike in this respect.

Evenings find Lucille in a state of profound anxiety. She calls, we speak. Sometimes I visit, stay. When I last saw her, she was much improved, less weeping, a communicable honoring of her lost child.

Like her brother and sometimes father, Bénédicte has vanished. No one knows where she is, not even—or especially—Anna, if Anna is to be believed. I've seen Anna, we've talked. She left me. The split was cordial. But not as cordial as it might have been had I been having an affair with someone other than Bénédicte. She probably would have celebrated an affair with Lucille, felt the sting for a mere few days, weeks, appreciating our friendship as she does, the pleasantness of Lucille. Lucille suggested I stay at her place for the time being but I didn't want to intrude. We see each other often, a kind of mutual consolation assembly.

The practical details bore me—my belongings, bills, settling up, decisions—but they have to be dealt with and I want Anna to be well. She isn't what most people who function in the everyday would call well. Her devastation lingers, haunts, really, she is no boulder after all, she is another torn person, surrounded by as much beauty as she can generate around her. The minimalism of what was our shared home, her dress reflecting that starkness, light, like and unlike her daughter. But still weathering missing family, the scaffolding of other people. I've taken note of the struggle, worn in her expression, the defensiveness of her body posture, with which she now accommodates my presence, when that presence is absolutely necessary.

Bénédicte is gone. I visited her apartment, it seemed as though no one had been there since her departure, her departure for Helsinki. Everything is mostly in order. Not the order of her mother, but clean, not immaculate, not matriarchal, but tidy, a lovely environment. I nearly cried there, again, at the thought of Bénédicte. That's twice, nearly three cries in several months, a personal record. Anna has decided to deal with the apartment. I'm going to miss it. I contemplate Bénédicte there, or moving through places we've occupied together, she's in my thoughts with great regularity. Perhaps she's gone to collect herself, a temporary reprieve, she may return, to me, to us, though I doubt it. We've done a horrible thing. We've deceived a mother and a life partner. I thought about this life just after having seen Anna a few days ago, likely the last time for a while. I still encourage her, desire her wellbeing, love her, I never stopped, that is life to me. I enjoy her company less than I enjoy that of Bénédicte, who is probably not coming back to me. I hope she returns to Anna. I'm immensely hopeful for them.

The women in my life suffer, this is clear. They're not alone in their suffering, however, that's ridiculous. Some time ago I did something that had nothing to do with women. I witnessed an accident. A cyclist—there are many here, especially in the warmer months—was hit and probably killed. First, however, he was doored. Speeding down Avenue du Parc, there, in front of everyone, he collided with the car door at precisely the moment that it was nearly perpendicular to the body of the car, his bike bumped the door while his body flew, a bit too much to the left. The car behind him had no time, there was none, the driver braked but could only skid into and over the cyclist. It happens sometimes here, but not like this. Out of everyone, I was the first to run from the safety of the sidewalk, bend over the bleeding rider, speak to him, even though I was only speaking to mangled body, cracked everything, he was barely alive. He didn't look at me. There was no such cognizance, no such heart-stirring look between us that I'll never forget. He was just there, dying, and I could think of nothing to do but be with him. I stroked the stranger's forehead, still relatively smooth and unbloodied. I felt the hell of his predicament, and the naturalness of it all, a small semblance of equilibrium there.

But what I remember about being with him before the ambulance arrived—I don't know whether he survived, I'm doubtful—as I sit in my solitary, makeshift home, is this physical absence of his being, this moment of ontological weight, in contact with my own, my own being there, on the street. And the sensation of our bodies being locked into the same struggle to endure, to carry on even as we move towards extinction, death. The suffering of bodies. It becomes philosophy, as opposed to the concrete suffering of a cyclist hit, a mourning family, a stillborn child, I know. But anyone who thinks that philosophy—even mine, an amateur's—doesn't produce suffering is not alive in thought. I do, in fact, live with the dying concession of the cyclist. And now, in emotional if not physical proximity, with that of an incomplete mother. Two, in fact.

Anna has been acting. Onstage. She has embraced that lifestyle in the secret folds of her time away from me. And even before the airport. The degree to which it removes her from herself, temporarily, from the problems of her life and death, she says. The Grotowski method, Laban. L., as it turns out, is Laurent, as in Laurent the acting teacher. They have yet to sleep together. Good for her, I say. I mention off-handedly that I would like to attend a performance sometime, about which she remains absolutely silent, still.

Where I'm staying, until I settle on something more permanent, there are the usual amenities. I received an email from Kari this morning. I don't know how he found me—he is a detective—he invited us back any time. He called me his friend. I thought of asking him to track down Bénédicte but then thought better of it. Too intrusive. Too complicated. Anyway. It would be difficult from there. Tracking down Bénédicte from Finland.

I imagine Bénédicte in some other city, another country, staying with a friend, carefully evading the slow-moving guilt that must have begun to creep into her conscience by now. Not about Anna—that's been there from the beginning—but the guilt of having abandoned a routine. The way routines become like family, part of one's identity, a limb. I envisage her calibrating the poise of her typical demeanor alongside impulses to weep, to cave in to the ugliness of it all. But really—and this is another matter of philosophical debate, I know—the only tragedy is that we got caught, in that way. Not in bed—how ordinary, how truly vulgar that would have been in its ordinariness—but in love. At an airport, with bags. Otherwise, it would have all come to a head in a relatively ordered manner, one of us, me, probably, sitting down in the comfort of a home, away from air travel, holidays in the bitter cold, and explaining to my partner that life has shifted. A surprising development has occurred that will anger you, perhaps make you hate me, us, but in this and in any moment of calm, or explosion, I'm here to work through it with you. Had there been that level of order, things might be quite different now and Bénédicte might still be here, rather than lost to us, suffering in the way that I know, I know she is, wherever she happens to be. There is censure in her now, partly directed at me, but mostly herself, for having deserted us, everything. I've missed her as much as I thought I would.

Her countenance, intelligence, the many things she has taught me. I rarely think about her sexually, in the sense in which men tend to think about women as erotic objects. I do this on occasion, of course—of course—

but mostly I notice a difference between thinking and sensing her in this way, even when she's not around. The way our bodies have merged, the way bodies do this and thus resonate with one another in the larger sphere of life events. I rarely entertain images of her as an object, there's too much of her, the way she is in life, to be so reduced. Though when I do see her in this way, her body alone in the cavern of my thoughts, in a moment of respite from work, at my desk, or earlier, before the meltdown, in the neutral, generally unsexed bedroom next to Anna, I focus on the usual images. Her stomach, the gentle slopes of her thighs, legs on a park bench, I know the intricate workings of her sex, the folds and layers, the tight interior space between her legs that often became wet with me and mirrored the same wetness of her mother, who I also know. Breasts that are surely pleasing to anyone who has such a predilection.

I imagine her suffering from film withdrawal. Not having the access that she has here. She's different from me in this respect. I don't need film the way she does, I merely enjoy it when it's around, treat it like a fine novel, or a terrible novel—I'm reading even more these days— think it through, why it's atrocious or worthwhile, discuss it. Bénédicte actually enters the film. Even when the film presents a closed circuit, a dull formula, she finds her way into the film with her body, that sounds trite, but that's how it happens, a kind of meditation in the cinema, or, to a lesser degree, in the living room, in front of the television. She refuses to answer the phone during a film, will avoid urinating if at all possible. I remember when she first chided me for eating something crunchy in front of the television while a film was in progress. Maybe it's a cliché, a product of wishful thinking, to imagine that she's currently stepping off the screen, away from the actress, and living a more authentic life, however difficult that life may be. She may be even more ensconced in film now, away from our afternoons. She may even have joined the cast of her favorite film, contemplated the film's conclusion, where things generally work out between lovers, parents. But either way, I don't think there's any question about the authenticity of her life, the things she does, the impact she has on others. It's all very real. And often quite artful.

The view of downtown, from the hill that passes for a mountain in the center of the city, affords one a joyful experience. There are numerous vantage points from which to see the city, small enclaves for a few parked cars, the numerous forest trails, and everyone's favorite, the Kondiaronk Belvedere. One must contend with the tourists, Americans, but all the lives, architecture, the old university, literate people, impoverishment, pornography, the largeness of the city really comes alive from such vantage points as one gives oneself over to the view. One dislikes others less when given over to the spectacle of the city. There's a sense of community on the mountain, people leaning over the stone rail, having their pictures taken, people looking through the massive binoculars. Or perhaps one ventures inside the Belvedere, has a cup of hot chocolate, it's easier to be isolated there despite the people milling about, staying warm in the winter, children laughing in all seasons. The staff of the Belvedere can be a little distant and that's fine, one accepts distance and the overpriced hot chocolate in light of what otherwise amounts to obvious grandeur.

In the country, Lucille and I have enjoyed a break together. We drove slowly, stopped, took bathroom breaks, a driver's mindfulness of creatures crossing the street. We arrived at the chateau with plenty of time to spare before dinner. The proprietors were interested in the fact that I was there with another woman, but when I asked for a room with two beds, they seemed to understand. They understood nothing, really, the dramatic turn with Bénédicte, her mother, the miscarriage of Lucille, and it never occurred to me to inform them of these developments in our lives. They asked about the city, how things are in the city, it's much warmer out now and you can feel the lift in people, a different energy there, I said. They sometimes miss the city. I suggested that they have a nice life here, in nature. One of the proprietors made a funny but derogatory comment about marriage that his wife eschewed. I didn't blame her, it was too easy, that joke. But Lucille took it in stride and laughed. She remarked on how good it was to be amid greenery, natural sounds.

We left the chateau for dinner, after a pleasant walk in the wilderness. A little restaurant in a nearby town. They know me there as well. Lucille ordered this time. Everything on the menu is decent, vegetarian, thoughtful food. I have a toothache. At dinner she talked me through a program of upcoming events in her life. I asked about her last boyfriend and she dismissed him with a wave. There's nothing, she said. Our food arrived and she was less interested in hers than I was in mine, so we shared. I don't always know if she's being completely honest when she complains about her food. Sometimes I think she just wants to share plates, wanting as much variety as possible.

In the night, alone in our room, we appreciated the rustic quality of our quarters, the interior design that one might expect from such a space. Rich reds and browns, funny, country ornaments. But mostly tasteful, the proprietors are, after all, originally from the city. The painting above the bed was in fact reasonably unattractive. Lucille lying on the bed, fully clothed, though we were both feeling that it's nearly time to sleep, that we could continue our discussion, our time together, in the morning. My tooth continued to hurt. I removed my shoes, untucked my shirt. Sitting in a chair next to the bed.

The final comment that Lucille made before leaving to wash up in the bathroom was only mildly startling. She said that currently the eighth most popular English name for a baby girl is Addison, while for boys, number one is Aiden. How strange, she said, how names can designate a boy or a girl, how male and female names can be interchangeable. I raised my eyebrows to express curiosity and then glanced down at the floor, Lucille still standing there, in the doorway of the bathroom. I noticed an insect, some species of roach, crawling up my pants leg and didn't bother to swipe it away, allowed it to continue what appeared to be a very decisive trek upward. And took no small pleasure in the security of our mutual plight.

THOMAS PHILLIPS is the author of *Long Slow Distance*. In addition to writing fiction, he is known internationally as a composer and performer of minimalist electronic music. He has taught multidisciplinary courses on literature, music, and film at various universities in North America and Europe.

SPUYTEN DUYVIL

Meeting Eyes Bindery
Triton

Made in the USA
Las Vegas, NV
25 June 2023

73901011R00090